NOBODIES

ADVANCE PRAISE FOR NOBODIES

"Smart, sensitive, and deadpan, these stories make us feel both reassured and insecure. Serious while being tongue-in-cheek, perplexed while still authoritative, Gilmore pokes a playful innocent stick at the idea of who gets to tell a story and why. *Nobodies* is full of real talent: for straight-up realistic storytelling and the more inventive exercises in form."
~ Michael Winter, author of *Into the Blizzard*

"Chris Gilmore's portraits of wannabe somebodies finding their way through put-ons, come-ons and trying it on are movingly sensitive and wickedly satirical. The dialogue pops, while the daredevil experiments with narrative form rejuvenate storytelling in an age of texting, sexting, and Tinder. These are stories to put hair on your chest and then joyfully, tenderly rip it off."
~ Robert McGill, author of *Once We Had a Country*

"Timely and irreverent, *Nobodies* takes loving aim at our contemporary approach to sex and relationships, and explores what our changing attitudes to connecting mean for our psychology and our stories. With wit and insight, these formally playful stories skewer our strange modern world."
~ Grace O'Connell, author of *Magnified World*

"A truly disturbing, funny, and sharply observed take on loneliness, insecurity, and the search for connection through the omnipresent, semi-permeable barriers of modern hyperconnectedness (and excessive body hair). It will also remind you how many of your favourite writers died of tuberculosis."
~ Andrew Battershill, author of *Pillow*

NOBODIES

Stories

CHRIS GILMORE

Copyright © 2016 by Chris Gilmore

All rights reserved. No part of this book may be used or reproduced in any manner whatsoever without the prior written permission of the publisher, except in the case of brief quotations embodied in reviews.

Publisher's note: This book is a work of fiction. Names, characters, places and incidents are either the product of the author's imagination or are used fictitiously, and any resemblance to actual persons living or dead is entirely coincidental.

Library and Archives Canada Cataloguing in Publication

Gilmore, Chris, 1989–, author
Nobodies / Chris Gilmore.

Short stories.
ISBN 978-1-988098-22-7 (paperback)

I. Title.

PS8613.I499N63 2016   C813'.6   C2016-905033-5

Printed and bound in Canada on 100% recycled paper.

Now Or Never Publishing
#313, 1255 Seymour Street
Vancouver, British Columbia
Canada V6B 0H1

nonpublishing.com
Fighting Words.

We gratefully acknowledge the support of the Canada Council for the Arts and the British Columbia Arts Council for our publishing program.

to my parents

SOME OF THESE STORIES HAVE PREVIOUSLY APPEARED IN PRINT

Exhibit A, High Plains Register, October 2016
Cormac McCarthy Orders a Pizza, Matrix Magazine,
December 2015 (Journey Prize Nominee)
Ping Pong, Oxford Magazine, May 2015
The Incomprehensible Here, Goose: An Annual
Review of Short Fiction, April 2015
The Problem of Other Minds, The New Quarterly, May 2014
Writer's Block, Goose: An Annual
Review of Short Fiction, April 2014

Table of Contents

Shaving 3

My Coffee with Jim 17

Exhibit A 25

Exhibit B 43

The Problem of Other Minds 47

Writer's Block 59

The Love Song of J. Alfred Killoran 69

Tickle My Ear 91

Infamous Endings 127

Nobodies 131

(More) Infamous Endings 151

Cormac McCarthy Orders a Pizza 155

The Incomprehensible Here 159

Ping Pong 171

Faces 187

OKCupid For Dummies 195

The Librarian 215

Shaving

She said she hated hairy men. She was drunk at the time, but you could tell she meant it.

I'm a hairy man.

Our first date was forty-eight hours away.

I therefore had two days to make myself an un-hairy man.

If you recall, I'd been looking forward to this date for almost a year. When I met her at Derek's Christmas party, she was still seeing Jeremy. They'd been together for three years, and everyone assumed they'd get married. But I could tell she wasn't happy. The false smile, the fake laugh. She was clearly putting on an act. I gave the whole thing six more months. They lasted ten and a half.

When she finally dumped him—citing "irreconcilable differences"—I didn't swoop in immediately. I wanted to give her some time to recover, maybe even fool around a bit. The last thing I wanted to be was a rebound. So I waited a few weeks, then popped the question: WANNA GARB A DINK SOMETIME?

It was two in the morning when I sent the text. I knew I'd second-guess myself if I reread it, so I sent it as soon as I finished typing. For some reason caps lock was on, and autocorrect was off.

Regardless, her answer was yes. LOL sure, to be precise.

"Ugh. I hate hairy men."

Like I said, she was seven drinks in, but it didn't matter. The truth comes out when you're drunk.

I tried to stay positive, pretend I wasn't bothered, but my facade was probably transparent. For the rest of the evening I watched her gossip and giggle with Karl and Derek and Julie, the usual pub night crowd. I searched for things to say, ways to intervene in the conversation, but I couldn't come up with anything useful.

Before we parted ways, she gave me a hug and said, "Looking forward to Friday."

I replied with a half-hearted "Me too."

Then she smiled and walked away.

When I got home, I took off my shirt and stood in front of the mirror. Hair, hair, everywhere. My exes used to call my chest a "magic carpet," a "fuzzy blanket." God knows what *she* would call it.

Like most guys, I didn't know the first thing about hair removal. I wasn't one of those image-obsessed bros with leg-sized arms and a shiny six-pack. I had itty-bitty boy boobs and a beer belly. In twenty-four years, I'd gone to the gym twice, and one of those times was a tour.

Ugh. I hate hairy men.

Hate. She used the word hate.

She may have been exaggerating, but I couldn't risk throwing away a potentially life-changing relationship over something as silly as follicle status.

Waxing was out of the question, as was laser hair removal. The former was too painful, the latter too expensive. Both required appointments, and time was of the essence.

I went to the bathroom and stared at my razor. The blades, which seemed to be grinning at me, looked even sharper than usual.

Sleep on it, I told myself. Decide when you're sober.

I put on my shirt and returned to the living room. After a moment of hands-on-hips indecision, I walked over to the couch and lowered myself onto the leather. The cushion released a long *puffffff*.

I sat so still I could hear the clock ticking, the fridge humming, the wind whistling through the alley.

Ugh. I hate hairy men.

The words echoed in my mind like a mantra.

This was high school all over again. Alice McCarthy in grade ten. Caroline Roth in grade eleven. By grade twelve, rumors had spread, so I kept my shirt on until college.

I studied my reflection in the blank TV. Handsome with the shirt, hideous without. I imagined it melting away, strand by strand, exposing the jungle beneath. Thick near the nipples, wispy near the neck. Tangled and glossy, like vines. A thin trail from breast to navel, with a donut-sized patch above the belt.

Suddenly, the hair was gone too, and with it years of neglect. I had a pair of noteworthy pecs and the outlines of a burgeoning six-pack.

Without chest hair, my reflection told me, I would look like a model. Forget my date on Friday—I should shave it off, in any event. How did I not think of this before?

No, you moron. That's the beer talking. Don't do anything until you get a good night's rest.

Easier said than done, of course. I was completely wired.

I looked around the room in search of a distraction. Everything reminded me of my dilemma. The fuzzy miniature fern in the corner. The smooth, elegant curves of the couch. The crisp whiteness of the walls, unpolluted by lines or markings.

Eventually, I got up and grabbed a book off the shelf. I didn't know or care which one I'd selected. I just opened it to a random page near the middle and started reading. "The Hollow Men," by T.S. Eliot. One of my favorites.

> *We are the hairy men*
> *We are the stuffed men*

I snapped the book shut and put it back.

I took another off the shelf. *The Hairy Ape and Other Plays*. For seven seconds there was no one I hated more than Eugene O'Neill.

I pulled out another. *Notes From Underground*. Dostoevsky. Nothing about chest hair in this one.

I returned to the couch and flipped to the opening page:

> *I am a sick man . . . I am a hairy man.*

"Jesus!"

I threw the book across the room, knocking over the fern in the corner.

My apartment was telling me to shave—and shave now. I couldn't wait until morning. Whenever I shaved my face, it'd be sensitive, and I'd need a day to recover.

I pulled out my laptop and Googled "body shaving," only to get bombarded with porn sites. *Ebony Slut Shaves Her Friend. Naughty Step-Sister Gets A Trim. Eduardo Scissor-Hands.* And so on.

I put my laptop aside.

How hard can body shaving be? It's just like regular shaving, except everywhere.

I paused a moment, then sprang off the couch and marched to the bathroom. The razor's grin had disappeared. It must have known what was about to happen. For a second I even felt sorry for it. Imagine if *your* life consisted of chewing up hair and spitting it out. To use my beloved's expression, ugh.

After a few deep breaths, I ripped off my shirt and grabbed the razor. One hair at a time, I told myself. Just think about Friday.

Friday, Friday, Friday.

I inspected the depth and breadth of my magic carpet, unsure how or where to begin. I settled on the top left corner, where the chest meets the collar bone and the collar bone meets the shoulder. That way, if I gave up after three strokes, I could still salvage a decent look.

I closed my eyes and held the blade to my chest.

One, two, three—swipe!

In less than a second, a patch of inch-long hair was reduced to stubble. The razor held its remains with pride. As I brushed them off with my thumb and blew out the leftovers, I didn't bother aiming for the sink. There would be mountains of hair by the end of this exercise. I may as well use the floor.

Inhaling deeply, I raised the razor to my pec.

Friday, Friday, Friday.

Swipe!

And just like that, another patch was gone. No cuts or rashes. No irritation of any kind. Maybe this wouldn't be so bad. Maybe I'd even find a six-pack under all that foliage.

Probably not, but it was worth finding out.

So I continued, one stroke at a time, and soon the floor was spotted, Dalmatian-like.

It took forty minutes to finish the chest, ten of which were devoted to nipples. Afraid to slice them off, I held a finger over the areola and pulled the blade—very carefully—around the rim.

Shaving the rest of my chest was easy, relatively speaking, but it wasn't much fun. Every stroke made a scraping sound, as if I were peeling off a band-aid, and the more hair I lost, the less recognizable I became. After my boy boobs were bare, I looked not just alien, but *like* an alien.

That said, it was nice to see my belly button again. For nearly a decade it had been covered in hair, and I'd almost forgotten what it looked like.

When I was finished, I swept the hair into a fuzzy pile and dumped it in the toilet. All that anxiety, flushed away in a tiny swirl of brown.

I sized myself up in the mirror. Contrary to my hopes, I did not develop a six-pack. Nor were my pecs enhanced. If anything, I looked fatter than before. Flabbier.

My magic carpet had been aptly named. It gave my chest shape and definition. It filled out the fat-free area below my collar bone and filled in the muscle-free remainder. Above all, it made me look manly. And now it was gone.

I brushed the last specks of hair off my abdomen and put on my shirt. It felt weird. Not itchy, exactly, but strange, as though a thousand little needles were poking my skin. I wiggled around inside of it, trying to find a comfortable position.

This girl better be worth it, I found myself thinking.

I flicked off the light and went to bed.

When I woke up an hour later, my chest was on fire.

I ran to the bathroom and tore off my shirt. Red, from neck to navel.

I couldn't call the ambulance or go to the hospital. They'd mock me and send me home.

I looked at the clock. 1:58AM. None of my friends would be awake. And even if they were, I couldn't call them. My female friends would never stop laughing, and my male friends would stop being friends.

1:59AM. Forty-two hours until the most important date of my life, and I looked like a racist cartoon. When I went to bed, I may have resembled a giant baby, but at least I could function. Now, I couldn't even move without wincing.

Unable to look at myself any longer, I sat on the toilet and buried my head in my hands. The internet would probably only make things worse. My friends were enemies in this scenario. Who the hell could I ask for help?

My head shot up with the answer: Mom! I could call Mom! Night or day, she said to call if I was ever in trouble.

I rushed to the phone and dialled her number. Five rings before she answered, and when she answered, it wasn't in English.

"Hemmmo?" she mumbled, which I took to mean hello.

"Hey, Mom. It's me. Sorry to call so late."

"Arem you okkkay?" She was groggier than I expected.

"Well, no, to be honest. I'm—"

"Oh my God," she said, suddenly awake. "What happened?"

"I'm—"

"Are you in the hospital?"

"No."

"Are you in jail?"

"No, Mom. Calm down. I'm just—"

"Don't scare me like that! Jesus!"

"I didn't mean to startle you. I'm just having a bit of a problem, and I was hoping—"

"What kind of problem?"

"Um. Well . . ."

"What?" she asked, half-concerned, half-impatient. "What's going on?"

"Well, it's no big deal or anything, but I sort of . . ."

I couldn't tell her the truth. It was too shameful. But I needed to tell her something.

Suddenly, the perfect question popped into my head: "How do you shave your legs?"

"How do I what?"

"Shave your legs. How do you shave your legs?"

There was a long pause. "Why do you want to know?"

"I just do, okay? I just do. Don't ask me why."

She sighed. "Are you high again?"

"What? No."

"Don't call me when you're high. You know how I feel about marijuana."

"I'm not high, Mom. It's a serious question."

She asked if I was planning to shave my legs, if I was planning to shave someone else's legs, if I had already shaved my legs and something went wrong. No, no, and no.

Eventually, I broke down and told her what happened.

"Are you sure you're not high?"

"I'm not high, Mom."

"Are you drunk?"

My response was a long-winded sigh. "Can you just tell me what to do? I'm in a lot of pain here."

"Oh, relax. You'll be fine."

She recommended lotion. I told her I didn't have any.

"Well, you're stuck until morning then."

"Perfect."

She asked if I shaved my chest in the shower, if I used shaving cream, if I used water, and, once again, I answered with a string of Nos.

"Oh my God!" she screamed, bursting with laughter. "You probably scraped off your skin!"

She laughed for a solid twelve seconds. Genuine, uncontrollable laughter at her son's expense. Complete with howls and coughs near the end.

"I'm sorry, Sweetie," she said, calming herself down. "It *is* pretty funny though."

"I'm sure it is—to everyone else."

"Oh, it'll be okay. Just give it a day or so."

She asked how things were going, otherwise. I told her things were fine. She said she was glad to hear it and apologized again for laughing at my pain. We said good night and hung up.

By morning, the rash had improved. My chest was still red, but the painful burn had been replaced, mercifully, by an uncomfortable itch. I thanked God, the Fates—whoever was listening. I'd never been so grateful to be uncomfortable.

That is, until I stepped out of my boxers on the way to the shower and caught a glimpse of myself in the bathroom mirror. The bottom half of my body was two shades darker than the top! I had the pale, hairless chest of a Scandinavian twelve-year-old and the legs of a middle-aged Brazilian!

Along with my magic carpet, I concluded, I must have shaved off my tan. In one night, I'd gone from King Kong to King Kong Having An Identity Crisis.

I couldn't let her see me like this. If I thought things would go badly before, imagine how they'd go now. And it's not like I could cancel our date. God knows when I'd get another one.

I stared, eyes watering, at my reflection and drew the only possible conclusion: I'd have to shave my legs as well. Yes, I'd look like a child, but it was better than looking like a lunatic.

If only I was a competitive swimmer. I could've passed the whole thing off as a badge of athleticism. Instead, it was just a mark of insecurity.

I hopped in the shower and started shaving. This time, the hair slid off like it had never been attached in the first place. My legs were bare in fifteen minutes. As were my forearms. Yes, I decided to shave those, too.

I dried off and assessed the damage. As predicted, I looked like a boy whose balls hadn't dropped, but at least my look was consistent.

I left my pubes intact, for obvious reasons. I wanted to appear polished, not porn-ish.

And I'm not trying to brag, but in the right light, from the right angle, I kind of looked like a Greek god. Hairless, except for a tasteful pubic puff. Like the statue of David, with a decent-sized dick.

My legs felt strange—tingly, cool, oddly damp, as though I couldn't stop sweating. When I touched them, however, the skin was dry.

I got dressed and ran to the drug store across the street. Every time my skin touched cloth, it recoiled.

Twenty minutes later, I was lathered up, lying naked on the couch.

The leather stuck to my skin, but it was still more comfortable than wearing clothes. I just had to remember to keep my ball sack elevated, so it didn't get glued to the couch.

I looked at the clock. Thirty-one hours until the date. I closed my eyes and prayed to every deity I could think of. I atoned for my sins, gave thanks for my blessings, and begged for my suffering to stop.

Friday arrived with a whole new set of anxieties. What should I wear? What should I talk about? What if she doesn't show up? The usual pre-date worries.

Luckily, none of these concerns were hair-related. By 7:30PM the rash had faded, the itchiness had become tolerable, and the tingly sensation had been minimized by hourly applications of lotion. In less than a day I went through half of the bottle. And since I forgot to buy the unscented kind, I spent the day smelling like a flower shop.

By 7:59PM I was at the bar, ready to make history.

She was five minutes late, of course. Fashionably dressed, fashionably tardy. She wore her favourite blazer and a matching scarf. Think what you want, but she was herself, through and through.

When the waiter arrived, she ordered her usual, as did I. Then we started talking.

For a while, things went well—better than I'd expected. She even seemed nervous, and, for a moment, I wondered if she was as confident on the inside as she was on the outside. The thought passed quickly, and I returned to worshipping her every word, look, and gesture.

After eleven months of semi-friendship, things were finally starting to unfold as they were supposed to. That is, until I rolled up the sleeves of my sweater and she saw my hairless arms.

"What happened?" she asked, furrowing her brow.

"Oh, nothing. I just did a little shaving."

"You shaved your arms?"

"And other stuff too."

"Like what?"

"Oh, you know . . ." I could feel my hands starting to shake. "My chest . . . my legs . . ."

"Your legs?" A smile broke out on her face. She was trying hard not to laugh. "Why would you shave your legs?"

"Uh. Well . . ." I searched for the right words at the bottom of my glass, finding nothing but bubbles. "It was . . . something you said."

She didn't know what I was talking about.

"The other night. You said you hated hairy men."

She laughed. "I was drunk. You shouldn't take these things seriously."

I could feel my cheeks heating up. My pits were sweating, too. A wave of irritation swept over my skin, and I wanted nothing more than to go home and cover myself in lotion.

"For what it's worth," she said, "I don't hate hairy men. I was probably thinking of back hair. And nose hair. And all the other gross kinds of hair. Chest hair is fine. In fact, I kinda like it. Makes me feel like I'm fucking a man. Gives me something to hold onto."

I'd never heard her use the word fucking before. At least, not as a verb. It threw me off-balance. As did the image of her straddling some macho idiot with enough chest hair to grab.

"So you have *zero* body hair?" she asked, clearly astonished.

"Almost. I still have my pubes."

She laughed, harder than before, then held up a hand in apology.

She changed the subject, and for the next two hours we discussed the usual topics. Books. Movies. Current affairs.

Eventually, she went home, and I never saw her again. Romantically, I mean. I saw her, platonically, every Wednesday at pub night. And even though we seemed to get along, I could never quite tell how she felt about things.

When I'd texted her, three days after our date, she said she had a great time, but would rather be friends. She didn't say why, and I was too afraid to ask. But I always wondered.

Was it my lack of chest hair, leg hair, and arm hair?

Or was it the insecurity underlying that lack?

I never really found out. Maybe it had nothing to do with either. Maybe I said something offensive during our date. Maybe I should've walked her home. Or worn a sweater with un-rollable sleeves.

Maybe. Maybe not. I guess we'll never know.

My Coffee with Jim

Dr. BlahBlah, PhD Candidate
youraveragepostmodernhipster.blogspot.com
Posted: 4:44PM, 08/18/2014

Another date. Another disaster.

This time, with a decent guy. A guy I might actually see again.

We met for coffee after a few days of chatting online. Nothing too in-depth or risqué. Just the usual getting-to-know-you chit-chat.

First thing he said: "Hey, if you could live anywhere in Europe, where would it be?"

I was intrigued, mostly by what he didn't do. He didn't reference my breasts, my butt, or my looks in general. He didn't throw me a bullshit compliment. He didn't call me something stupid, like "gurl," "hot stuff," "sexy," "hoe," or "bitch." He didn't offer his dick on a platter. He asked me an interesting question. A question he probably copied and pasted 1000 times, but an interesting question nonetheless.

(In case you're curious, here are some of the comments I received today, from complete fucking strangers: "yo slut" (from *crazy_ballz69*, whose interests include "chillin" and "pimpin"), "what colour r ur nipples? send pics" (from *donkeypuncher*, who seems to enjoy posing shirtless beside his Honda Civic while wearing sunglasses and a backwards hat), and "whaddya say?" accompanied by a blurry picture of what looks like a penis but might be a mouldy hotdog (from *Hoe_Fsho*, who claims to know "the secret to keeping bitches happy"). There are literally 56 others (just as bad or worse) that I could include, but you get the picture.)

So I reply, for no particular reason, "Amsterdam."

And he tells me about his vacation two years ago when he went to Amsterdam and saw the Anne Frank house and visited the Van Gogh Museum and smoked weed at this coffee shop in the Red Light District, etc. etc. etc.

So I ask him (jokingly) if he hooked up with any prostitutes while he was there.

And he says "No lol Of course not" and then a few minutes later adds a long paragraph saying he doesn't have anything against prostitutes and thinks their profession is completely respectable and legitimate as long as it is well-regulated and there is no coercion or mistreatment involved, and then a few minutes after that he sends another paragraph claiming that he feels unable to reconcile his feminist inclinations with the implicit objectification that prostitution would entail even if such objectification is consensual and the agency of the prostitute in question has not been compromised.

So I tell him I was joking.

And he says he knew that, but he wanted to make his position clear anyway, just for the record.

So I say okay.

And he says okay. And he asks if I'd like to grab coffee.

Before I say yes, I double-check his profile. Self-summary: refreshingly bland. No bragging, no self-absorption, short and sweet, with a dash of humility and a hint of humour. Goals: admirable. Interests: acceptable. He likes (more or less) the same bands, the same shows, the same authors. (The fact that he even reads is a plus these days ...) And under *I spend a lot of time thinking about* he writes, "how much time I waste when I think about how much time I waste." Not bad, right? Overall assessment: decent guy.

(And his pictures are cute. No sunglasses. No backwards hat. No Honda Civic.)

So I say yes, and we grab coffee, and everything goes well until we get to the park ...

(I just realized that I probably shouldn't mention his real name. Or mine, for that matter. Let's call him Jim. And we'll call me Jan. And we'll call the other girl Jen. Okay. Here we go.)

I guess it all starts at the picnic bench when he asks, *How's OKCupid treating you?* Not bad, I tell him. Better than Plenty of

Fish. *Yeah, I tried that one too. How long did you last?* A few weeks. *You?* A few hours. Too many creepy messages. *I can imagine.* Apparently I look like I'm sixteen. And apparently that's a good thing. *According to who?* Men over 30. *Jesus.* One guy wanted me to get on Skype and eat a cookie. *Like a chocolate chip cookie?* I think he asked for oatmeal raisin. [Jim laughs.] *Suddenly, I feel so much better about myself.* You should. You're not a pedophile. *I'll drink to that.* [He raises his cup.] Cheers. [We clink cups and drink.] *I have to say, I was impressed by your movie list.* Why, thank you. *I noticed you're a Woody Allen fan.* Oh . . . Yeah. Kind of. *Midnight in Paris . . . Vicky Christina . . .* I made the account a while ago. *You don't like them anymore?* No, I do. I'm just . . . I'm trying to avoid his films these days . . . given all that's happened. *You mean the Dylan Farrow thing?* Yeah. I feel like I shouldn't support him anymore. *Ah.* You disagree. *Well . . . I mean, whatever he did doesn't change the fact that Annie Hall is a great film. Or Manhattan.* Or I can't watch Manhattan anymore. The thing with the high school girl . . . *You mean Tracy? She's almost legal.* [He can tell that I'm offended.] *I'm not saying it's okay. I'm just* "She's <u>almost</u> legal?" *You know what I'm saying.* It sounds like you're saying statutory is fine n' dandy. *I'm saying it's complicated.* Oh boy . . . *I'm saying—first of all, it's a movie. Okay? Tracy is a fictional character.* His daughter isn't. *Adopted daughter.* I can't believe you're defending him. *I'm not defending him. I'm just* Mansplaining him. *We have testimony, okay? Not facts. He said, she said.* I think Dylan's story is pretty convincing. *And I think Allen's story is convincing. That's the point. All we can do is speculate.* Because Mia dropped the case. *And why do you think that is?* It's obvious. She didn't want Dylan dragged through the *That didn't stop her from using her in court in the first place.* "Using her in court?" She was molested for Christ's sake! *Again, that hasn't been proven.* You're such a guy. Defending the heroic male artist, whatever the consequences. *And you're such a girl. Defending the wounded female victim.* Don't call me a girl. *Don't call me a guy.* What should I call you then? *I don't know. Jim works for me.* Fine. *What's your name again?* [I respond with my best bitch face.] *I'm kidding. Jesus.* I think I should go. *Come on, I didn't mean to* Offend me? *Just . . . Please? I'm sorry, okay? We're just talking. That's all. Just chatting.* [He desperately searches for something to say.] *What are your thoughts on ISIS?* [I sigh.] *Better question: What was the last good book you read?* Gender Trouble. *Oh, right. You're in Women's Studies.* And you're a filmmaker. *Well, I don't know about "filmmaker" . . .* That's what it said on your profile. [I take out my phone and start reading.] "Aspiring filmmaker. I'll show you my short film if you show me yours." *Riiiiiight . . . How short is "short"?* Uh . . . about average. Five, six minutes? *Seven, actually. Eight, with the credits.* What's it about? *Oh, you know . . . this and that.* What's your thesis on? *Misogyny in mainstream American culture.* Ah. That makes sense. *What makes sense?* Uh, you know, the whole Woody Allen thing. *No wonder you feel so strongly* So I have to be a women's studies major to feel strongly about a child molester. <u>Alleged</u> *child* [I let out a rage-filled sigh.] *Look, I'm not saying I want him to baby-sit my kids.* You don't have any kids. *How do you know?* What are their names again? *I'm just trying to make a point.* About your hypothetical kids. *About hypocrisy. About our society's obsession with scandals and our inability to empathize* With pedophiles? Yeah. No empathy whatsoever. *Even if you're right: let's say he's a horrible human being who should be locked away forever—is it really our business?* Yes. *Why?* Fifty years ago, that wouldn't be the case. *Public figures* Public figures are people. They're not animals in a zoo. *What about politicians?* Politicians are politicians. Artists are artists. And artists are above the law. *You know what I mean.* So if you raped me right now, I should still pay to see your short film? *Woah! Okay there . . .* Hypothetically. *Jesus . . .* I know how much you like hypotheticals. *I like arguments that make sense, not inflammatory character assassinations.* You like well-reasoned viewpoints that aren't biased by personal experience. *Exactly.* Regardless of how relevant that experience might be. *It tends to distort more than it clarifies.* I see. *I'm sensing sarcasm.* No, not at all. I'm finally aware of my subjective bias, of how my personal experience has distorted my perspective. *What personal experience?* Oh, no, it doesn't matter. *No, really, I'm curious.* [I look away, trying to seem nervous.] *You don't have to tell me if you don't want to, but* My sister was molested. [He's speechless.] She was twelve. Her gym teacher . . . *My God. I'm sorry.* So you can see why I'm . . . *Yeah.*

Completely. I'm so sorry. [A long silence.] So now my perspective's valid? *Hmm?* It wasn't a minute ago, but now that I have a personal investment *Well, if your sister was molested* . . . I don't have a sister. *What?* Another hypothetical. *You don't have a sister.* Nope. *You're fucking crazy.* No more than most. *You're just like Farrow.* Which one? *Does it matter? They're both fucking nuts.* [I let loose a wide, wonderful grin.] Now who's the judgmental one? *I think I'm going to go.* Why? We're having so much fun. [He looks at his phone, pretending to check the time.] *I have a lot of things to do.* But I want to keep talking about hypocrisy and my inability to empathize. [He avoids my gaze.] Or the creepy guy from OKCupid. Remember? The one who made you feel so much better about yourself? We could talk about him, if you'd like. [He hangs his head.] Or we could talk about your short film. You still haven't told me what it's about. [He opens his mouth to speak, but nothing comes out. He looks down at his cup, then into the distance.] *It's about online dating. It's called "My Coffee with Jen."* Autobiographical? *Based on true events.* OKCupid or Plenty of Fish? *Plenty of Fish.* Uh-oh. *It didn't go well.* Was it better than this one? *About the same.* Did you see her again? *What do you think?* [I smile enigmatically and finish my coffee.] We should do this again sometime. [He furrows his brow, truly surprised.] *What are you up to this weekend?* Work. Writing. Drinking. *You want to see a movie?* Sure. Which one? *Can't remember the title. But I like the director.* Anyone I'd know? [He grins.] *Oh, I think so.*

Exhibit A

Tuesday, May 24—3:34am

Hello Stranger!

It was so good to see you tonight. (Or last night. Technically, the party was last night, but I think we actually spoke around midnight. I spotted you earlier, but the night really began—for me—when we started talking.) I loved what you said about meeting new people: how it's exciting and scary at the same time, how you never quite know who someone is or what they're capable of until you've spent some quality time with them. It's so true. There's always another layer to peel back and peek beneath . . .

Would you like to spend some quality time with me this weekend? My schedule is pretty flexible, so whenever works for you will probably work for me.

Sincerely,
Samantha Dorkins

Wednesday, May 25—6:37pm

I'm really sorry, but I just remembered that I'm having brunch with my mother on Saturday. I also have an archery lesson at 3 and a movie premiere at 5:30. (The premiere shouldn't take too long. A half-hour, tops. I just want to see Ryan Gosling walk the red carpet.) Which means, unfortunately, I'm only free in the evening. Sunday is still open, however. Sorry for any inconvenience, and thanks for understanding.

Thursday, May 26—7:03pm

Did you get my email about this weekend? I don't mean to rush you, but if you could respond ASAP I'd appreciate it. My friend Kimmy asked me if I'm free on Sunday for a Mario Kart Nacho Party, and I said I'd have to get back to her.

7:08pm

P.S. In case you're curious, a Mario Kart Nacho Party is not much of a party. (Otherwise, I'd happily invite you.) We basically just play Mario Kart and eat nachos. Whoever passes out first loses. To be honest, it's more of a competition than a party.

8:53pm

by the way, i just wanted to mention that you look so much better in person. the camera must add like fifty pounds, because you looked sooooooo dammmmn goooood the other night. just sayin.

8:59pm

(sorry, ive had a few drinks.)

9:01pm

i think i have a d-mailing problem. (drunk e-mailing.) i should have a designated typer! hahahahaha

okay then. signing off for the night. talk to you soon.

9:06pm

sorry, i just realized my "better looking in person/fifty pounds" comment (from my email sent at 8:53) could be misinterpreted. i didnt mean you normally (or even sometimes) look bad. youre hot. perma-hot. youre so hot, im surprised youre not on fire. literally. someone should set you on fire, just to prove my point. (tee-hee.)

9:08PM

PS i apologise for the "hahahahaha" (in my email sent at 9:01). as i said, ive had a few drinks. and i forgot to take my meds this evening. its no big deal, but i sometimes get a little nutzo if i dont strike the right balance.

9:09PM

oh, and in regards to my "someone should set you on fire" comment (from my email sent at 9:06), i didnt mean someone should literally set you on fire. even though i literally said literally. im not an arsonist. just so we're clear on that.

9:14PM

and in case you were wondering, i got your email address from the bald guy by the bar, the one who kept staring at you. he said he was a friend of elaines, and elaine knew marty (your agent), and marty had given it to elaine. so dont worry. i didnt steal it, or find it online, or have someone killed. im legit, and the person who gave it to me is legit, and so are the people who gave it to him . . . but i cant blame you for being careful. there are a lot of crazy people out there.

9:16PM

just for the record, i dont think youre crazy. ive been watching the news, and (as usual) the folks at cnn have blown this way out of proportion. i mean, yes, you were driving pretty fast in a residential area, and, yes, you did have a blood alcohol level of 0.2, and, sure, you almost killed an old lady on her porch, but who hasnt made mistakes in their life? everyones so judgmental these days . . .

9:30PM

random question: is F & F as great as people think? or does it just remind you how alone and impoverished you really are?

9:38PM

(F & F means fame and fortune, by the way.)

9:43PM

this is a little embarrassing, but i have a poster of you in my bedroom, and my mother wants me to take it down. she doesnt think its healthy for a twenty six year old woman to have a poster of a movie star, but i told her youre an artist, and artists deserve to be worshipped, and if she touches it ill put her in a home.

anyway, thats all for tonight. sweet dreams. xoxo

9:45PM

in case youre curious, its the poster from "gravedigger blues." the one where youre shirtless, holding the shovel, with the zombies in the background. i have a few posters from "blinker" and "desdemona drunk" that show off your . . . other qualities, but i like this one for the badass look.

9:46PM

PS i noticed your jeans in the "gravedigger blues" poster have an unusually large bulge below the belt . . . ive heard people stuff socks down there to enhance their manhood, but im sure your manhood is mucho plump, sans-sock ;)

Friday, May 27—9:30am

I owe you an apology. I just read my d-mails from last night, and I can't believe what I wrote. I'm so embarrassed. I have a tendency to drink after a long day, and since I'm a lightweight, I have a tendency to get drunk . . . Anyway, I hope you can forgive my silliness.

Sam

10:46am

I forgot to mention when we met how much your work means to me. I was just so flustered and star-struck. (I don't meet my heroes very often!) To put things mildly, your movies remind me why movies are made. I know that sounds clichéd, but it's true. I don't know how you do what you do, but you do it better than anyone else, so please keep doing it. "Blinker" was incredible, my first cinematic love, and you somehow managed to top it with "Desdemona Drunk." Then "Catalyst," then "Gravedigger Blues," then "The Rusty Bulb." Each one better than the last. "The Rusty Bulb," especially. Don't listen to the critics. I didn't think it was pretentious, indulgent, derivative, and pseudo-intellectual. Or "Catalyst" for that matter. I'm not sure why people thought your accent was off. I'm no expert—I've never been to Bulgaria—but it worked for me! And your tour-de-force performance in "Gravedigger." Unbelievable. How the hell did you pull that off? And how did you not get an Oscar nomination, let alone a statue? My God. Don't even get me started on the Academy. It's all politics. They're just afraid to support an actor with a criminal record. (I thought that verdict was BS too by the way. Six months with no parole? That judge was on a power trip. He just wanted to make an example of you.) Fuck the haters, man. Fuck em.

6:27PM

(I hope this is the right email address. I mean, the bald guy just wrote it down on a napkin, and his writing isn't that great. I haven't received one of those delivery failure notifications yet, so I'm going to assume everything's fine. footlong_sub@gmail.com seems a bit generic for someone of your stature, but the bald guy seemed pretty confident about Elaine and Marty, so if someone screwed up, it was probably them, not the bald guy. Although the bald guy was pretty drunk, so who knows . . .)

SATURDAY, MAY 28—5:45AM

i was just reading the youtube comments for your charlie rose interview . . . i thought what killa877 said about your nose was disgusting. and hollabackgurlllll. christ, what a bitch. dont listen to those creeps. bigbooty69 was so right. your elbows are lovely.

10:32AM

Hey, sorry about the message from last night. (Or, more accurately, this morning.) I need to stop drinking after work.

10:34AM

I hope I didn't offend you somehow or scare you off. I promise I'm a normal, sane person. If you're not up for hanging out, that's fine, but please let me know either way. I'll totally respect your decision.

3:46PM

I googled your email address along with your name, and I discovered, after four hours of digging, that footlong_sub@gmail.com is the right email address after all. Which means you're ignoring me. Like most people, I don't enjoy being ignored. It's rude and uncalled for, and I think I'm entitled to an apology. Or, at the very least, a response.

3:49PM

Look, I can understand why you'd be apprehensive about corresponding with someone who is practically a stranger. But I'm not a stranger. We shared a genuine moment at that party. Yes, it only lasted a few minutes, but they were minutes that meant something. With you, a few seconds is more than enough. And I know you felt the same thing.

So what do you say? How about we grab a coffee and go from there?

SUNDAY, MAY 29—3:47PM

I'm not very impressed by how you're handling this . . .

5:09PM

I'm not mad. I'm just a bit frustrated that you won't respond. I mean, it's basic common courtesy. I don't mind being rejected, but I can't stand being ignored. So tell me to go away. Tell me to piss off. I don't care. Just tell me something.

5:10PM

Better yet, don't tell me anything. Reply with a blank message. That way, at least I'll know you're listening.

8:34PM

You're really not going to respond, are you? Why? What the hell did I say that was soooooooo horrible?

8:57PM

Look, I'm sorry, okay? Can we start over? I'm just having a bad day. Some hobo threw a McFlurry at me.

9:04PM

I mean, in the grand scheme of things, this is all so silly. Maybe it'll be one of those stories we tell our kids!

9:05PM

(Haha. Jk. Wink. (Actually, I'm not kidding. (Don't worry, I'm totally kidding . . .)))

11:14PM

What do I have to say to get you to respond? I've already apologized. You want me to call you names? You want me to threaten you? If you want me to act like a lunatic, I will. Not a problem. You seem to have me all figured out. I'm more than happy to conform to your assumptions. You know what? I'll even start drinking. Give me ten minutes, and I'll come back wasted. Then we'll see who's ready to talk.

11:43PM

apologies, im a few minutes late. those last few shots didnt go down so well . . .

where was i? oh yeah. acting crazy. you know what? im too tired for this shit. lets pick it up again in the morning.

sleep well, dick.

Monday, May 30—10:04am

Okay, I'm back! Well-rested, sober, and ready to go!

Before I dive into the personal stuff, I'd just like to say a few things . . .

Over the course of our correspondence, I may have given you the impression that I admire your work. If that's the case, I sincerely apologize, and I'd like to take this opportunity to clarify my position.

Point 1: You suck.

Sure, your early stuff was okay. I'm big enough to admit that. But GOD was it overrated. I mean, yeah, "Blinker" was decent. The scene with the driving instructor, the speech about bagels, the ear plug montage—all good stuff. The scuba sequence was a little contrived, but still enjoyable. The pool hall scene, on the other hand . . . What the hell were you thinking? And don't blame the script or the director. You fucked up and you know it. Everyone knows it. But you have a pretty face and a cute butt, so we all forgave you.

Point 2: You're not a director.

Case and point: "The Rusty Bulb." Who told you that was a good idea? You can hardly act, and now you want to direct? Who do you think you are? Orson Welles? Get off your high horse and join the rest of us on Earth. You remember Earth? That place where you used to pick up your pay check? Come back to it. (Actually, don't. No one misses you.)

Christ, just thinking about "The Rusty Bulb" makes me want to punch an orphan. What a pile of pretentious, indulgent, derivative, pseudo-intellectual trash. More importantly, what a waste of fifteen bucks. Not to mention two hours of my life. (Two-and-a-half, if you include travel time.) I still don't know how that piece of shit got into Cannes ...

Correction: I know exactly how it got into Cannes. Nepotism. Your name. That's it. No artistic merit. Just Hollywood clout. Well, I've got news for you: not everything you say and think and do is brilliant. In fact, most of it (around 98 percent) is total garbage, and you might want to take that into consideration before you get behind another camera.

Point 3: You're full of shit.

You pretend to be this great humanitarian, but your charity gives like ten bucks to African kids. (I looked it up.) You're worse than an asshole, my friend. You're a fraud. You're a fucking scam-artist. I hope you realize that, because if you don't you should see a doctor. Delusions of that magnitude are dangerous.

10:48AM

P.S. I take back what I said about the "unusually large bulge" on my poster. It's totally photoshopped, not to mention sock-stuffed ...

10:52AM

P.P.S. I saw that picture in US Weekly, the one taken at the beach ... (And don't blame it on shrinkage. Water's cold, but it's not THAT cold.)

11:23AM

What, no comeback?

11:25AM

Come on. You're no fun.

11:34AM

Fine. Whatever. I'm done.

Have a nice life, asshole.

1:12PM

And don't even bother apologizing. I'm not going to listen. You had your chance, and you blew it. (Don't say I didn't warn you.)

1:46PM

Hey, did you just try to email me? I got an email from fizzlecrackerrrr@hotmail.com, and it was blank. Are you fizzlecrackerrrr? And, if so, would you mind saying a bit more than nothing?

1:48PM

I replied to the fizzlecrackerrrr message, just in case it's from you. I don't know why you'd reply with a different account and leave your message blank, but I'm sure you have your reasons . . . (Or maybe you're not fizzlecrackerrrr, in which case I owe fizzlecrackerrrr an apology . . .)

2:31PM

fizzlecrackerrrr just replied. He/she offered me a free trip to the Bahamas. All I have to do is give him/her my credit card information . . .

2:58PM

Still not talking, eh? Have it your way.

8:54PM

its your loss. im doing just fine without you. youre the one with the meaningless life. who cares how much money you make? if anything, F & F just makes life harder . . .

8:57PM

you know what? im glad youre turning me down. im actually grateful. youre probably needy and clingy and insecure, and thats the last thing i need right now . . .

9:12PM

i actually understand you. do you realize how rare that is? in this messed up world? to find someone who really understands you?

im not even mad anymore. i just feel bad for you. im sexy and smart and accomplished, and i have tons of friends (probably more than you), and everyone i know worships the ground I walk on. im not just a pretty face. i actually have a soul. i have a mind. im the complete fucking package.

seriously. you should see the guys ive slept with . . . i wont name names. im above that gossipy shit. but theyre big. (and i mean big in every sense of the word, mr sock-stuffer . . .)

9:14PM

i could tell you if you really want to know, but youd have to promise not to tell anyone. two of them have been in movies with you . . .

9:16PM

do you want to know? ill tell you if you really want to know, but you have to ask.

9:24PM

okay then. youre loss. i guess youll just have to wonder for the rest of your life . . .

9:27PM

ill give you a hint. one of them has the initials J. P. any guesses?

9:32PM

(now, im just trying to fill up your inbox . . . im surprised you havent blocked me yet.)

9:34PM

wanna do a shot?

9:35PM

no? okay, more for me. seven and counting . . .

9:36PM

i know where you live btw. just fyi.

9:39PM

kidding.

10:18PM

hey is it ok if we just start over and pretend this whole conversation didnt happen? im willing to forgive and forget if you are.

10:20PM

look i really want us to be friends. if you dont want to go out with me thats okay. no biggie. but i really want us to be pals. we get along so well and we have so much in common and i really think we could be super awesome BFFs :)

10:22PM

but seriously it would be sooooo great if we could go out. just once. just to try it. i know you wont regret it. my fortune teller said were meant to be together. and shes always right. ive been seeing her for three months and she hasnt been wrong once. even my mother thinks we would make a nice couple. she said so last week. and my friends think so too. most of them anyway. kimmy doesnt think youre that hot but shes dating a guy in a wheelchair so what the hell does she know.

11:23PM

okay heres the deal if you say nothing when i say what im saying now that means you like me and you want to go out with me

11:24PM

yaaaaaay you didnt say anything so that means you like me yaaaaay so when do you wanna go out

11:27PM

tomorrow the next day the day after that

11:34PM

WHY WONT YOU TALK TO MEEEEEEEEEEEEEEEEEEE

11:35PM

sorry didnt mean to use caps i should really stop drinking so much im up to shot #12 and beer #3 i think its time for beddy what are you doing tomorrow wanna grab a hot dog or something

11:37PM

you know what im hungry now i really want chow mein and chocolate for some reason is that weird

TUESDAY, MAY 31—12:04AM

i cant believe youre still ignoring me how dare you do you even know who i am i could end your career with one phone call i know a guy from high school whos super powerful and connected all i would need to do is call him up and tell him that i think youre an asshole and poof there goes your life

12:16AM

you know i wasnt kidding about knowing where you live if you wont talk to me here ill come to your house and talk to you there how does that sound

12:23AM

its a nice night for a drive i think ill go out for a bit

12:24AM

okay im leaving any last words

12:26AM

i want to forgive you i really do but youre making it very hard if you would just say something everything would be okay

12:27AM

last chance sweetie

EXHIBIT B

The following pages from Samantha Dorkin's journal (entitled "Conquests") were found in her basement behind the drier, next to a jar filled with hair samples and used condoms, each bearing the name of one of the following famous actors in permanent black marker.

JAMES FRANCO

Met at his place. Gave me a tour. Showed me his PhD, his paintings, his poetry book, his novel, his short story book, his one-man experimental performance art collage, "The Metatheatrical Selfie." (Didn't get it. Just a wall full of shirtless selfies.) Showed me the empty shelf where he plans to put his Oscar, his Pulitzers ("one for fiction, one for drama, one for poetry") and his Nobel Peace Prize.

Smoked weed. Talked about the books he wants to adapt. To Kill a Mockingbird "from the perspective of the mockingbird." Don Quixote "set in Vegas." Talked about all the gay poets he still wants to play. "Ginsberg and Hard Crane were just the beginning." "Isn't Hard Crane a porn star?" Shook his head. Asked if I wanted to see the broken tower. "Maybe later. Let's get drunk first." "It's better sober." "Don't say that. I'm sure it's great either way." (It wasn't.)

COLIN FARRELL

A true gentleman. Paid for movie, paid for dinner, paid for coke. Pledged to do a good film some day. "What about In Bruges?" "In what?" "You got a Golden Globe for it." "Ah right. Sorry. Memory's a tad spotty. I've been high since Alexander."

Played Truth or Dare. Dared me to braid his eyebrows. Then confessed secret lifelong dream "to accumulate millions while maintaining the lowest average Rotten Tomatoes score in history." Worried about competition from Kevin Costner and Michael Bay.

Joaquin Phoenix

Called me at 5AM, weeping into the phone. Called again at 7AM to confirm our date.

Picked me up at noon. Didn't recognize him without the beard and glasses. Brought flowers with a card. ("Get Well Soon, Auntie Martha.") Didn't ask where he got them.

Went drinking. Went driving. Almost hit a few kids but no one saw. (Totally their fault for being on the sidewalk.)

Dropped acid at Burger King. Drove around the parking lot, searching for God. Found Him under a Volvo, playing chess with a squirrel.

Made out in J's car. Asked him to rap. He rapped. Asked him to stop. He stopped. Stuck his gum on my shoe.

Drove home. A lovely, police-free afternoon. No breathalysers. No handcuffs. At least till we got back to my place ;) lolz

To-Do List

Miley
Beebs
The Guy From the Dos Equis Commercials

The Problem of Other Minds

As John counted his pamphlets, he noticed the blackbird slice its way through the smog, aim for the unlucky office on the seventh floor, collide, rebound, twirl, and land on the gum-spattered sidewalk no more than two feet from his mentor, Jonathan Swift. No one else seemed to notice the bird's death, so John finished counting and began reaching out, one pamphlet at a time, to whoever seemed open to new ideas. But the question of whether the accident was in fact accidental—and, if not, why a bird would choose to end its life—lingered in the back of his mind.

Without looking up from his newspaper, Swift brushed two finger-length feathers off his coat, felt his wig for other unwelcomed objects, and mumbled something that sounded like "Pity." John half-expected him to complain that he had just bought the coat, that this was the only wig he had, but Swift had once declared that understatement was a more dignified form of irony than sarcasm.

Car horns muffled the brushing of suits, the hailing of cabs, the clatter of high heels on the pavement, but John could still hear vacant sighs mourning their lost dreams and panicked phone monologues clutching those about to slip away. When he offered pamphlets to his people, his arm felt like a streetlamp shining a firm, proud light into the darkness of modern life. Swift said it would only make the darkness darker and cast a shadow on anything in its path. As usual, John couldn't tell whether Swift was being ironic. He could detect neither sarcasm nor understatement in his mentor's prophecy.

The outstretched pamphlet swayed in the breeze of human traffic, searching for a new owner, while the banner, taped to the marble wall behind him, fluttered and rippled, distorting its message: SUICIDE: A MODEST PROPOSAL.

"This will change your life," John said, "I promise." His targets were unconvinced. He'd lost count of his rejections, his lives unsaved.

Swift shook his head, eyes fixed on his paper. "Did you know that only one in fifty people admit to reading philosophy or 'philosophy-related' books these days?"

"You don't need to suffer . . ."

Swift turned the page. "It's criminal."

"Change your . . ."

A well-dressed brunette made an impolite gesture as she passed. John's streetlamp went limp.

"And this," Swift continued, "'The number of drug-related deaths and probable suicides has doubled in the past year and a half.'"

A model-thin businesswoman approached. John's streetlamp rose. "Make the right decision," he said.

"Go fuck yourself."

"Half of the country is on anti-depressants," Swift grumbled. "The other half is on meth."

John couldn't ignore this latest statistic.

"Oh, I wasn't quoting," Swift clarified. "That was just my two cents."

John wondered, given the choice, which half of the country he would prefer to join. "This can solve your problems . . ."

"Like they haven't heard that before."

John turned to chide his mentor, but something soft brushed his hand and took the pamphlet.

"Thanks," the girl said, tossing him a greeting card smile as she walked away. No older than twenty, she moved as though she had owned life from the moment she joined it.

At least one person would be saved today.

John watched her sunny blonde hair blend into the sea of black and white until its rays were completely obscured by suits.

Then he returned to his mission.

"Change your life," he sighed. "End the pain . . ."

Swift's newspaper crackled as he turned the page. "You look ridiculous," he stated, without looking up. "You know that, don't you?"

"I'm open to suggestions, Dr. Swift."

"Give the people what they want."

"Drugs?"

"Better than drugs."

John had deciphered these puzzles before.

"Who are you talking to?" a strange voice asked.

John spun around to find an ancient, bearded blob of a man sitting on the ground with a baseball cap between his legs.

"How long have you been there?" John asked, looking to Swift for guidance.

"Long enough to know you're crazy," the man replied. "Who's Dr. Swift?"

John pointed to his mentor, but the man seemed to look right past him.

Swift extended his pale hand. "Jonathan Swift, at your service. How do you do, sir?"

The man did not move. His skeptical gaze remained fixed on John, who glared at the man in disbelief.

"Well?" John said. "Shake his hand. Don't be rude."

The man's eyes widened, then narrowed, like he had answered his own internal question. He stood slowly, picked up his hat, and walked away. He looked back every few seconds, then turned the corner and disappeared.

"Lunatic," John muttered.

"You never answered my question," Swift said, reopening his newspaper. "What do people want more than drugs?"

"Happiness. Love."

"You're getting warmer."

John raised his arms and shouted, "Free money!" The syllables echoed through the crowd, turning heads in an instant.

"That works, I suppose."

John could not reload fast enough. "Free money . . ." He did not even need to raise his voice; the news travelled in desperate murmurs.

The frenzy even drew the attention of his mentor. "Any prophet will tell you: Providence arrives in numbers."

"Let's just hope they read them."

"Let's hope they *understand* them."

John's smile vanished. He looked to Swift for reassurance, but he had already returned his attention to the day's headlines. Swift never had much faith in people, but John was an optimist. He turned back to his people and propped up his smile.

"I'm sure they will."

★ ★ ★

It was not the apartment of a philosopher. Since he moved in three years ago—after his parents kicked him out and his last and only girlfriend left him—John had accumulated a coffee table with uneven legs, a couch with a missing cushion, and two wooden chairs, each more than twice the age of its owner. He had borrowed from his parents (without any intention of returning) a temperamental TV, an equally troublesome shotgun, and a variety of prescription drugs that he never took but kept nearby for peace of mind. John had crafted a shrine in the corner of his bedroom for Swift, who never failed to remind his protégé that one side of his mattress had become two inches higher than the other and that it smelled of false hope and wasted potential. Swift sometimes occupied the higher half of the bed—fully clothed and wide awake, lying stiff as a corpse—in an effort to increase its aesthetic appeal and remind John that a 300-year-old man with a wig was the closest thing to a woman the mattress had seen in nearly a year. Whenever Swift lifted himself off, however, the two-inch discrepancy remained, as if he had never been there at all.

The key turned in the rusty lock, the handle jiggled, and when the door felt just the right amount of weight, it flew open, enlarging the dent in the wall behind it. John entered his home—for the first time in months—with pride, while his mentor followed with only a smirk and a fresh cup of tea.

John threw himself onto the couch and sighed, breathing in the mouldy smell of success. Swift remained standing, arms folded, leaning against the room's only pillar, which divided the kitchen from the living room, the living room from the foyer, and the foyer from the kitchen. John assumed it was merely decorative. Such a narrow support couldn't possibly hold up an entire apartment, even one as puny as his own. A crack had recently formed down the middle of the pillar, and John half-expected the slightest tap to bring it down.

"Congratulations," Swift declared, watching John move to the kitchen. "I think you finally proved your parents wrong. Philosophers are not just lazy lunatics."

"We're life-changers."

"Whether the lives need changing or not."

John emerged from the kitchen with a bottle of beer.

"How many pamphlets did you hand out today?"

"I lost count. Over a hundred, probably."

"A hundred lives: permanently, irreversibly, irrevocably changed." Swift raised his cup. "Well done, sir."

John turned on the TV, only to find a news screen littered with familiar faces.

"Tomorrow," Swift added proudly, "we'll get even more."

John's curiosity morphed into shock as he recognized the greeting card smile and its glossy blonde frame.

"Wasn't she . . ." John mumbled, pointing at the screen. He turned up the volume. The anchorwoman announced that Susie Fields, aged nineteen, was one of numerous confirmed suicide victims, that the cause of the sudden increase in suicides remained unknown, but police suspected that the final toll might be over thirty.

John stood slowly, covering his mouth, then backed away from the TV, nearly tripping over a pile of books. Without spilling his tea, Swift emptied a bag full of old Chinese food onto the coffee table and handed it to John, who leaned on the couch for support. The bag ballooned in and out as he gasped for breath.

"Do you mind?" Swift snapped. "I'm trying to hear how many people you've killed."

John started moaning.

"Oh, don't worry. I'm sure they just misinterpreted your message."

John tossed the bag on the table and reached into his knapsack. He pulled out the remaining pamphlets and opened the one on top.

"'Life is bullshit. Kill yourself immediately.' That's the first fucking line!"

John threw the pamphlet at the wall and began pacing.

"And if they kept reading," Swift replied calmly, "they would have read the life-affirming conclusion. They would understand the irony—"

"Clearly they didn't!"

"Well, if they're too lazy to read a five-page pamphlet . . ."

John stopped pacing. "I'm a mass-murderer," he mumbled in disbelief. "I killed thirty people today."

"Well, according to the TV, it might be more than . . ."

John picked up the bag and held it to his mouth.

"Relax, you didn't kill anyone."

John lowered the bag, glaring at Swift.

"You just put the gun in their hand. You didn't pull the trigger."

John raised the bag and started breathing.

"Where all those people found access to guns, I'll never know . . ."

"You're not helping," John groaned.

"You're right. They probably used knives or rope or something. Electrocution, asphyxiation, poisoning, bleeding—there are lots of ways to kill yourself."

John leaned against the pillar for support. Swift began counting the methods on his fingers: "Jumping off a building, drug overdose, hair drier in the bathtub, cutting your wrists in the bathtub, drowning in the bathtub . . ." He turned to John with a smile. "Suddenly, taking a bath sounds like a dangerous proposition." He turned back to the TV. "I wonder what method little Susie used . . ."

John rushed into his tiny kitchen, opened the cabinet beneath the sink, and removed his father's shotgun. He then returned to the living room, sat in one of his antique wooden chairs, and put the barrel in his mouth. His finger hovered above the trigger. "Is this how you're supposed to do it? Like this?"

"This is one area where my expertise is limited."

"I should just copy the guy from that movie."

"Don't forget the pamphlets."

"Huh?"

"What happens when the police come? They find you, they find the pamphlets, they *read* the pamphlets . . ."

"Jesus."

John put down the shotgun, marched to the table, and grabbed the stack of pamphlets. Swift couldn't help but smile, watching John scramble through every drawer and cupboard, dig through discarded wrappers, dry pens, and rusted silverware, in search of a lighter. Swift cleared his throat and pointed to the fire extinguisher by the stove. John reached behind the dusty appliance to find an equally dusty pack of matches.

He dumped the pamphlets in his tiny bathtub and set them on fire. They burned faster than he expected. Head against the sink, he looked down at his life's work as though he blamed his people for the pamphlets' fate.

"You won't do much good to anyone dead, you know." Swift was now sitting cross-legged on the toilet, blowing on a fresh cup of tea.

"At least I won't do any harm."

The last embers of the pamphlets curled and cracked, spitting out a few last sparks of wisdom.

"If you deprive people of good, you're doing them harm."

John ignored his mentor's comment and slouched his way to the chair. He picked up the shotgun and resumed his original position.

"You missed one." Swift pointed to the pamphlet on the floor.

John picked it up and gazed at it like a father seeing, for the first and last time, his stillborn child. He recognized his turns of phrase, his cheeky wisdom, his all-too-elaborate sentence structures, but he could tell by its creases and faded ink—by the way it fell back over his hand like a rag doll—that this was a child beyond saving.

"Read the last line," Swift ordered.

John opened the pamphlet to the last page and cleared his throat. "The only answer to the question 'Why bother living?' is this: 'I have nothing better to do.'"

John lowered the pamphlet.

"Exactly. You have nothing better to do."

John raised the gun.

"The world needs you, John. They need to hear the truth. They need to be saved—"

"From what?"

Swift grinned.

"That's what I thought." John's mouth opened and the barrel slid in.

"If you give up now—you said it yourself—you're a mass-murderer. Not to mention, a coward. Don't forget your own message: suicide is never the solution."

"There are exceptions to every rule."

"If you continue your project . . ."

John's finger twitched on the trigger. Pools of guilt collected at the edges of his eyes. "They . . ." His voice trembled and cracked. Swift offered his handkerchief, but John shook his head. "They didn't understand me."

"They *will* understand you." Swift leaned forward and placed a hand on John's knee. "New ideas take time. All movements have growing pains. Think of Susie. Poor 19-year-old Susie Fields will have died in vain if—"

"Susie would want me dead. Susie's friends . . ."

"Susie would want you to do the right thing. Susie would want you to change the world. To make a difference in people's lives—"

"I already *have* made a difference."

Swift regained his upright posture, his unsparing tone. "When you look back, years from now, and you're famous, and worshipped, and everyone comes to you for guidance, what will you think?"

"When I'm famous . . ."

"You'll think Susie was a hero, just like all the others on that screen." He pointed at the muted TV, flashing pictures of the victims. "She's a martyr. Somewhere up there, wherever she is, she's happy. Because she knows she died for a worthy cause, and soon her parents and friends will know it too. Susie's just the beginning."

"If I take out the irony," John sniffled. "Make it easier to understand . . ."

"That's one approach, certainly."

"I'll rewrite it completely."

"Yes."

"Tailor it to the average reader."

"But the average reader . . ."

"What?"

Swift met his protégé's gaze with a gentle smile. "Are they really worth saving?" John's brow furrowed. "Don't get me wrong, they're nice people and all, but think about it: they don't care about questions of life and death. All they would do—assuming they even read it—is misinterpret the meaning, abuse their newfound wisdom, or disregard it completely." He pointed to the silent TV. "You saw what the 'average reader' looks like. These people are part of the problem, not the solution. Half won't even read your work, the other half won't understand it, and half of *them* will most likely use it for evil!"

John did the math. "So that leaves a quarter?"

"A quarter of the human race, able and willing to embrace your message." His humane smile resurfaced. "Do we really need the other three?"

"We *do* have a population crisis . . ."

"Raise the irony. Increase the difficulty. Make it as inaccessible as possible, and let natural selection do its job. The best and brightest will rise to the occasion, and the rest . . . will be the rest."

"Raise the irony . . ."

"Sacrifices must be made for the common good. Any leader will tell you that."

"Increase the difficulty . . ."

"Humanity needs a hero, John. Not another coward or another 'average reader.' We have plenty of those already. Humanity needs a leader."

Feeling the force of his mentor's vision—a spotless empire of sanity, courage, and happiness—John wiped his eyes and sprang off the chair, nearly dropping the shotgun on his mentor's foot. After testing a few pens on the back of his only remaining pamphlet, John found one with ink and began mapping out his brave new world.

"We'll increase the irony . . . make it completely inaccessible . . . maybe even write some of it in Latin . . ."

"Can't do any harm."

"Maybe we can even put little cyanide tablets inside, you know, to really test their willpower."

"No argument here."

"Once they understand the message—*if* they understand the message—it will be that much more rewarding."

"Absolutely."

"And if they don't survive the message . . ."

"The loss is no disaster."

John stopped writing and turned to his mentor. "Ready to save the world, Dr. Swift?"

"One suicide at a time."

Writer's Block

You want to write, but you have nothing to say. It's been proven. By family and friends and exes. You're too Canadian to complain. Too young, too spoiled, too boring. You haven't lived. You haven't lost. You haven't suffered. Your only complaint is that you have no complaints.

So you write about writing. About trying to write. You try to write about trying to write. And you fail.

First, you try on a few styles, hoping to find one that fits:

Ernest Hemingway
It had started to rain. She sat at her desk and stared at the blank page in the typewriter. She thought about the style she would use for her story and about her favourite writers and their styles. She got up and grabbed a bottle of beer from the refrigerator and poured the beer in a glass that had been sitting on the shelf beside another glass. She drank the beer. Then she put down the glass and walked back to her desk and sat in her chair. She wrote a fine and true first sentence.

Charles Dickens
It was the best of sentences; it was the worst of sentences.

Henry James
On a most devastating, tumultuous night, she sat poised over the page like a clenched wild dog, a vicious beast of an almost indescribable quality, until—frustrated by that most distressing, demoralizing, and disheartening of ailments: writer's block—she swiftly stood, approached the cabinet, poured herself a large (but not embarrassingly large) glass of that undignified amber drink, returned to her study, rolled up her elegant sleeve and—dispelling every distraction, every counter-productive thought—began to

write her monumental (though slightly awkward and ill-conceived) first sentence.

WILLIAM SHAKESPEARE
Shall I compare thee to a starting line?
Thou art more clumsy and more [three-syllable adjective]

T.S. ELIOT
Writing is the cruellest art, breeding
Tired narratives out of old experiences, mixing
Metaphors and similes, stirring
Readers' expectations with dull plots.

Speaking of plots, you think of a good one. Predictable, but reliable.
    You start a vomit draft. No names, no settings. Just outlines. Arcs. Shapes.

J. woke up and
    [insert activity]
Usually, she would
    [insert routine, background information]
[This new activity] allowed her to
    [insert positive internal developments resulting from external developments]
and J. felt that everything would be
    [insert optimistic platitudes, foreshadowing symbolic significance of new activity]
J. wondered what [Love Interest 1] would think of [this new activity] considering
    [insert Conflict 1: unrequited love]
J. concluded that [Love Interest 1] would be unimpressed, as always, but
    [insert Conflict 2: inability to accept rejection]
J.'s family and friends felt
    [insert Conflict 3: disapproval of Love Interest 1]
and begged J. to pursue other men.

You stop to refill your glass. And stretch. And brainstorm the end of Act One.

What does J. want? you ask yourself, as if expecting to know the answer.

J. wants what everyone wants. A good story, well-told. In which she is the central character.

What do you want? you ask the page, as if expecting to read the answer.

The page replies, I want what you want.

J. always wanted
    [insert comic anecdote about minor obstacle]
but she never
    [insert pathetic ending to comic anecdote about minor obstacle]
However, today J. finally overcame [minor obstacle] and vowed to ignore
    [insert Conflict 4: social, political, familial influences]
as well as
    [insert Conflict 5: influences beyond her control: fate, circumstance, the will of the Gods]
She would, from this day forward, always
    [insert resolution towards self-actualization]
by
    [insert distinguished determination to determine and distinguish between distinguishing factors of pre-determined distinction and distinctive non-deterministic factors within her determination]
But all that goes without saying.
    [insert conversational, self-conscious, self-deprecating remark, breaking illusion of narratorial authority and objectivity to illicit reader's sympathy through ironic admission of (false) humility]

And what I want, you tell yourself, is poetry. Life-altering, life-affirming poetry. On the page and on the stage. In mind. In body. In action.

Poem 1: "Aesthetics"

Art for its own sake
is ~~never always~~ never out-of-date.
(At least, not at this rate.)

Poem 2: "A Poem Whose Title Is Longer Than the Poem"

Is not worth reading.
Or writing.
And (starting now) the title is misleading.
The lies deepen with every word.
Every syl la ble.
Every l e t t e r.
Every .

Poem 3: "Forty Seven Words for Snow"

I read somewhere
That Inuits have

Forty seven
Different words to describe

Forty seven
Different types of snow.

I thought this would be
A good subject for a poem.

But I'm not sure
Where to go with it.

(I have to stop now.
That's forty seven words.)

You love words but have no clue what to do with them. Like boys. You worship from afar. You fantasize. Idolize. Romanticize. Someone should tell you: when you worship, you belittle. When you approach, you retreat. Words won't love you unless you let them. Unless you think you're worthy of their affection. Words fear you more than you fear them. Like boys.

Your story isn't working. Even the page can tell. You need to write something real. Something personal. Start small and expand. Forget plot. Forget story. Start with a sentence. An idea. Hell, start with a verb. All you need is a word. And a boy. In that order.

Start with a sentence. A style.

JAMES JOYCE
First sentence. Not the second. Second can't come till the first. Sounds philosophical. Philosophicale. Pale ale. Good for the glands. Good for the soul. Writing equals soul. Soul equals glands. Glands swollen. Soul swollen. Soul-swilling sloshing soul-swabbing sipping. Yes. Good first sentence. Will write. Yes.

LEO TOLSTOY
All good first sentences are alike; all bad first sentences are bad in their own way.

WILLIAM CARLOS WILLIAMS
so much depends
upon

a good first
sentence

written with authority
and power

beside the other
sentences.

William Faulkner

because if it could just be the two of us me and the first sentence in some hell somewhere and I could do something dreadful I would say *Father I have committed plagiarism it was not my first sentence it was someone else's*

Samuel Beckett

No words. Never words. Blank page. Blank pen. Blank mind.

First wine. Then words. First word. First sentence.

Go on. Can't go on. Go on.

So
   [insert return to main narrative, apology for digression]
J. called [Love Interest 1] to tell him
   [insert internal developments (which were inspired by external developments) and external developments (which were inspired by internal developments)]
 [Love Interest 1] asked why J. was really calling.
   [insert J.'s rambling, unconvincing response]
Unconvinced by her rambling response, [Love Interest 1] hung up.
   [insert J.'s despair]
Walking down the street,
   [insert plot twist: chance encounter with Love Interest 2, followed by clichéd conversation, number exchange, and successful first date]
J. was
   [insert happiness]
After a few months of dating, J. introduced [Love Interest 2] to her family and friends.
   [insert Conflict 6: disapproval of Love Interest 2]
J. disowned her family and rejected her friends, but eventually
   [insert Conflict 7: disturbing discovery about Love Interest 2, confirming suspicions of family and friends]
J.'s relationship with [Love Interest 2]
   [insert gradual decline of affection, resulting in break-up]

Poem 4: "Dear Diary"

What would you do
with Love Interest 2,
considering that 1
was not very fun?

Should I look for 3
or possibly 4?
Should I forget about 2
and struggle no more?

Seeking guidance, J.
    [insert unsuccessful phone calls to friends and family]
Then, seeking comfort, J.
    [insert unsuccessful phone call to Love Interest 1]
Then, seeking wisdom, J.
    [insert alcohol consumption]
Then, seeking the sweet relief of death, J.
    [insert time-consuming search for accessible bridges and tall buildings]
J. puked in an alley, blacked out on a bus, and woke up in jail with bruises and a hangover.
    [insert recovery]
A week later, J. called [Love Interest 2] and apologized.
    [insert melodramatic, cathartic conversation]
J. and [Love Interest 2] agreed to try again.
    [insert optimistic moral message]
But
    [insert pessimistic moral message to override optimistic moral message]
J. and [Love Interest 2] were finally
    [insert ironic, unrealistic happy ending]

Poem 5: "Untitled"

Sorry.

I couldn't
think of anything
clever.

How about
this:

Poem 6: "Writer's Block"

[leave space blank]

The Love Song of J. Alfred Killoran

"Women will never love you," my brother informed me, "unless you know how to tame them." Frank opened his textbook to a page entitled 'Mating Habits of the Lowland Gorillas' and slid it across the lunch table. "See what I mean?"

"No."

He pointed to a gorilla: chest puffed, fists clenched, teeth bared. "What do you have in common with him?"

"Nothing."

"Exactly. If you want Cindy to like you, you have to look like him."

"I don't have any chest hair."

"I'm not talking about chest hair, Jeff." He closed the textbook. "I'm talking about seduction. I'm talking about control. If the man's not in control, he's not a man."

Were you in control of Emily, I wanted to ask, *when she dumped you for the football moron?*

"There's a science to it," he continued. "You have to treat it like an experiment. Research, prepare, analyze—"

"Sounds romantic."

"You want my help or not?"

"I'm still waiting to hear something helpful."

He took a deep breath and cleared his throat. "Okay, Casanova, listen carefully . . ." *Twelfth graders think they have all the answers.* "If you want to get girls—if you want to get Cindy—you have to have the mind of a gorilla to go with the body."

Emily's new boyfriend certainly fit these criteria. Perhaps Frank was onto something.

***

Experiment 1: The Gospel According to Frank

Plan A: Staring (a.k.a. "Alpha-male") [1]

QUESTION: Will Cindy respond favourably if I stare at her in class?

HYPOTHESIS: Yes.

PROCEDURE:
1. Enter classroom.
2. Sit in assigned seat.
3. Stare at Cindy.

VARIABLES:
a) She responds positively: smiles, winks, blows kiss, etc.
b) She responds negatively: throws something, tells teacher, tells police, etc.
c) She does not notice.

RESULTS: She did not notice.

CONCLUSION: Attempt *Plan B*.

★★★

"And if staring doesn't seem to work," Frank added, "she's only testing your perseverance. That's when you become aggressive, like the gorillas."

"Are you suggesting I punch her?"

"That would probably get her attention."

"What if she punches back?"

"She's a girl. It won't hurt."

"Is that how you got Emily to like you?"

---

[1] "The quickest way to a girl's heart is to let her know as soon and as often as possible how much you care about her. Stare at her long enough, without blinking or moving, and she'll be yours." (Frank Killoran, 03/05/2001)

"I didn't need to punch her. I just got her drunk."

"Do you have any wine I can borrow?"

"Look. You just have to remind her that you're the most important person in her life, whether she's aware of it or not."

"What if she doesn't want me to be—"

"All girls want you to be, trust me. They love whoever loves them the most."

"I guess that's only fair."

"Oh, yeah. Girls are always fair when it comes to love. It's like a sport to them."

"So I guess the football moron loved Emily more than you did."

He looked away. "I guess so."

"Otherwise, you'd still be dating."

"That's right."

"And she'd still love you."

"Something like that."

DIGRESSION:

> For all his encouragement, Frank never had much faith in me. Whenever he could, he'd remind me how Cindy was out of my league, how *he* would have a better chance of wooing her, how after two years of pining the best I could hope for was the girl in math class with the lazy eye. Whenever Cindy would pass us in the hall, Frank would pat me on the back and say, "Go get 'em, champ," like a patronizing father who is all too aware of his son's limitations.

★★★

Plan B: Aggression (a.k.a. "Primal Dominance")

QUESTION: Will Cindy respond favourably to some form of physical assault? [2]

---

[2] "It is a scientific fact that women are attracted to aggressive men. That's why Emily dumped me: I wasn't aggressive enough. But I have a feeling her new boyfriend is keeping her satisfied." (Frank Killoran, 03/05/2001)

HYPOTHESIS: No.

    SUB-QUESTIONS: a) Is Frank an idiot?
                                   b) Is Frank deliberately misleading me?

    SUB-HYPOTHESES: a) Yes and b) Possibly.

PROCEDURE: 1. Enter classroom.
                       2. Sit in assigned seat.
                       3. Gauge Cindy's mood.
                       4. If neutral/negative, punch her shoulder.
                       5. Ask her out.

    SUB-PROCEDURE: After execution of *Plan B*, interrogate Frank concerning his intentions/loyalty. If results are suspicious, disown Frank.

VARIABLES: Too many to count.

RESULT: Experiment abandoned.

CONCLUSIONS: Confirmed cowardice.
                      Consider *Plan C*.

★★★

"If punching doesn't work, I have one more idea."
    "You'd like to see me in prison, wouldn't you?"
    "If it works for gorillas, it'll work for you."
    "Prison?"
    "No, my plan."
    "Oh."
    "It's complicated, so pay attention . . ."

★★★

Plan C: Sensual Movement (a.k.a. "Mating Dance")

QUESTION: Why bother?

HYPOTHESIS: No clue.

PROCEDURE: (Cannot remember steps.)

RESULT: N/A

CONCLUSION: Spared dignity.

★★★

"You're out of options, Jeff."

"No, I'm out of *your* options."

"Don't blame me if Cindy doesn't like you. She's allowed, you know."

"Was Emily allowed?" [3]

"After a suitable period of time, yes."

I studied his stoic green eyes, his poker face lips, searching for signs of duplicity.

"Are you trying to screw things up with Cindy?" I finally asked.

"What?"

"Don't lie to me."

"I'm your brother. Why would I do that?"

"Because you're my brother."

★★★

---

[3] After Emily broke up with Frank, he drove by her house, honking and howling her name, every night at the same time for two weeks. On the last night, a police car was waiting for him. Frank's best friend, Anthony, told me this story. He heard it from his friend Dale, whose locker is next to Emily's. So it must be true.

EXPERIMENT 2: THE GOSPEL ACCORDING TO JEFF

Plan A: The Sensitive Poet [4]

HYPOTHESIS: Contrary to Frank's "alpha male" approach, and based on the romantic films I've seen, women frequently seem fascinated by tortured, sensitive men. Therefore, if I appear "dark" and "mysterious," Cindy will most likely develop feelings for me.

PROCEDURE: 1. Try to emulate the "sensitive poet" mystique: brood, weep, moan, etc.
2. Write her a poem.

RESULTS: After hitting Cindy in the back of the neck with a piece of eraser (to get her attention), I tossed my folded-up poem at the foot of her desk. She read it, smiled, and tucked it into her notebook.

DIGRESSION:

> I borrowed my mother's poetry anthology and scanned the table of contents for a poem with "Love" in the title. I found a "Love Song" and changed the title, so Cindy couldn't trace the poem to its original source. I copied out the first few chunks, but I cut the silly line about a patient on a table.

The bell rang. Cindy walked over to my desk.
"Would you like to ask me something?"
"Well . . ." I mumbled, "I thought we could . . ."

---

[4] If this doesn't work, *Plan B* is called *The Comedian*. "Girls like guys who can make them laugh," my father always said. But he never made my mother laugh, and she didn't seem to like him very much, so I never knew whether he was speaking from romanticized memories or theoretical speculations. *The Comedian* is my contingency plan, because, like my father, I'm not very funny.

"Yes?"

"You like movies?"

"Yeah . . ."

"There are some good ones coming out this weekend, if you wanted to go . . ."

"With you?"

Adopt gorilla persona. "Got anything better to do?"

"Uh, yeah, I'm—"

"What?"

"I'm . . ." She seemed baffled, caught off-guard. "When did you want to go?"

Shift to poet persona. "Whenever."

"How about Friday?"

"Sure," I said, shrugging.

"My dad can drive us."

I let my eyelids droop with indifference.

She tore off a piece of paper and wrote something on it. "Give me a call," she said, handing it to me. (My hand was shaking, but she didn't seem to notice.) "See you later," she added, waving as she walked away.

★★★

I must have examined that piece of paper every five minutes until our date, half-expecting it to dissolve if I didn't confirm its existence. Above her phone number, beside her pink bubble-lettered name, whose "y" wore a delightful swoop, she had drawn a tiny heart. It was a simple shape—two curved pink lines, linked symmetrically—that solved all of life's mysteries.

DIGRESSION:

> Months later, in a fit of rage, I threw Cindy's pink heart out the window, only to run into the street and find it had blown away. For weeks afterwards, I examined any shred of discarded paper, hoping to recover the only thing Cindy had ever given me. I considered asking her to rewrite her name and number, but the heart

would doubtless be absent. (And even if she did include a new one, it wouldn't be the same as the first.) Eventually, I found a pink pen and tore off a few corners of paper—never getting the shape quite right—but I stopped writing Cindy's name after the first three sloppy letters. I could never copy her adorable "y," so I didn't bother trying. Nor did I attempt to reproduce her pink heart.

★★★

"So what?"
"What do you mean 'so what'?"
"It's just a heart."
"It's not just a—"
"It's a heart, Jeff. You have to focus."
"It's a signal."
"It's a line on a paper."
"Technically, it's two lines—"
"She's not in love with you."
"That's your opinion."
"You're going out in an hour. If you want to survive, listen up."

I swallowed my pride along with the half-dozen rebuttals I wanted to throw at him. "I'm all ears, Frank. You always know best."

★★★

Experiment 3: First Date

Problem 1:	Cindy was supposed to pick me up five minutes ago.
Explanation:	If she arrived on time, she would appear desperate and over-eager.
Conclusion:	Don't be paranoid.
Problem 2:	Cindy was supposed to pick me up fifteen minutes ago.

EXPLANATIONS:	Unlikely:

                              a) Fatal accident.
                              b) Fatal illness.
                              c) Traffic.

                        Likely:

                              a) She had been mocking me in class and has no interest in dating me.
                              b) She has forgotten our date completely.
                              c) She is being deliberately coy/evasive.
                              d) She is just plain rude and has no sense of common courtesy.
                              e) She is too cowardly (or kind) to reject me in person and accepted the date with no intention of keeping it.
                              f) She is clinically insane.

RESPONSE: Call her and tell her she's a self-absorbed sadist who will never be happy until she realizes that being beautiful does not give her carte blanche to be cruel.

RESULTS: She would break out of her cocoon of narcissism and become a decent human being. She would owe her future happiness to my courageous confrontation and even come to love me for it. We would tell our grandchildren this story, and teach them life's most valuable lesson: if you want something badly enough, you can always get it.

CONCLUSION: I must confront this goddess, who (as I consider more carefully) is anything but divine. At best, she is a frail human being, like me, but more likely a demon sent by Satan to torture boys.

I marched to the phone, and just as I finished dialing her number, the doorbell rang.

Cindy's father made sure I sat in the back seat alone, while his daughter rode in comfort and safety beside him. His gaze shifted in the rear-view mirror from the traffic to me so often I wanted to remind him to watch the road. But I kept my mouth shut, as all good future sons-in-law should.

Her father broke the silence. "So Cindy tells me you're in her English class. How do you like it?"

"I don't."

"Why is that?"

"I like science. Books are . . ."

"Stupid?" Cindy suggested.

"Exactly. Stupid."

Her father met my gaze in the rear-view mirror. "I'm a librarian."

"Oh."

"Are you reading Shakespeare yet?"

"No, thank God."

He frowned. Cindy laughed.

DIGRESSION:

> I made her laugh! What were a man's greatest attributes in the eyes of women, according to my father? Good looks, a soul, a brain, and a sense of humour—in that order. I was (and am) unremarkable in the looks department; my soul and brain were under construction—planned completion time: still unknown—but the existence of my levity-brevity organ had finally been confirmed, and by the only person whose opinion mattered.

Her father did not like uncomfortable silences. "So aside from science, what are your interests?"

"Uh, I'm not really sure . . ."

"How do you like to spend your free time?"

Masturbating, mostly. "Oh, you know. The usual ways."

"Such as?"

"Just lying around . . . letting my mind wander."

"Until it finds something it likes."

Or until Mom asks why the door is locked. "Yeah. Something like that."

"Ah, the power of imagination. Fantasy. I suppose when you're fifteen, that's all you have."

Not anymore.

"Separate or together?" the cashier asked.

How did Frank not cover movie date etiquette? [5]

"Together," I croaked. Afraid to make eye contact with Cindy, I handed the cashier a quivering twenty dollar bill, which my parents had given me for the occasion.

"You didn't have to do that, you know."

"It's okay," I said, handing her a ticket. "You can get it next time."

Cindy quickened her pace, and I felt a vague tension nudge its way between us. Was she upset because I paid for her ticket or because we missed the previews?

Say something to gauge her feelings.

"Do you want any snacks?" I asked.

It's a shame when the first thing to enter your mind is the first thing to exit your mouth.

QUESTIONS:
1. Who is paying?
2. How much is she entitled to get?
3. Does "snacks" necessarily include a beverage, or just food?
4. Since I already paid for the tickets, is she now obligated to buy me food?
5. Does she feel coerced, manipulated, deceived?

---

[5] Frank and I discussed more general first date skills: how to start fights with anyone, man or woman, who seems attracted to Cindy ("Girls love over-protective guys. It makes them feel safer."); choosing conversation topics that lead to discussions about yourself ("Girls don't like talking about themselves. They want to learn about you."); the appropriate length of time to stare at Cindy's breasts ("Three seconds is acceptable. Any less and she'll be insulted.") and so on.

"No, I'm all right," she said, tucking an errant strand of blonde behind her ear.

"I think I'm going to get something."

Slow learner.

EXPERIMENT 4: MOVIE WATCHING ETIQUETTE

PROBLEM 1: THE POPCORN

OPTIONS:
a) Hold the popcorn on my lap.
b) Reach around the armrest and balance it on my knee, tilting it in her direction.
c) Give it to her to hold.

QUESTIONS:
1. Does she even want any popcorn?
2. Am I obligated to share?
3. Is sharing considered an insult somehow?
4. If I give her the bag to hold, will she assume it's for her and wonder why I bought her something that she explicitly said she didn't want?
5. If I keep it on my lap, will she assume I don't want to share with her?

I balanced the bag on my knee, hoping she would take the hint, but she didn't even glance at it. After four minutes, my wrist became sore from holding the bag at an angle, so I returned it to my lap. Just when I'd given up, she reached over—without looking away from the screen—and pulled out a handful of popcorn.

PROBLEM 2: THE COKE [6]

QUESTIONS:
1. Since I got her a straw of her own, does that imply that I like her enough to want her to share

---

[6] When I bought the Coke, I had asked for a second straw in case Cindy wanted to share, but I didn't put it in the cup. Sharing popcorn was innocent, but there was an unspoken intimacy in sharing your Coke.

| | my Coke, but not enough to share my straw? |
| | 2. Does a single straw suggest that she isn't welcome to share, or that I'm putting her in the awkward position of embracing my straw germs before she's ready? |

RESULT: When I stuck the single, lonely straw through the top, she didn't seem to notice.

CONCLUSION: Add another variable: Insert the second straw.

RESULT: Status quo.

CONCLUSION: Draw her attention to the second straw: Tap her somewhere.

OPTIONS: a) The shoulder? Too awkward in this position.
b) The forearm? Too intimate.
c) The hand? Way too intimate.
d) The knee? Too odd.

After a dozen deliberations and false-starts, I used more force than necessary and thrust my finger into her shoulder. I forced my lips into what I hoped resembled a smile and pointed to the second straw in the Coke. She glanced at it, unimpressed, then turned back to the screen. I looked around to ensure that no one else had witnessed my blunder, and to my delight everyone seemed as engrossed in the awful film as Cindy.

Despite its ridiculous premise,[7] the film grabbed my attention when the protagonist kissed his love-interest for the first time. I looked to my fellow moviegoers for guidance. A nearby teenaged couple were entangled together, while the elderly pair in front of us appeared to be asleep. The middle-aged couple a few rows down were sitting straight in their seats, and, as far as I could tell, they hadn't moved since we arrived.

---

[7] A man is obsessed with a woman who has no interest in him, but, completely unaware, he pursues her anyway.

I glanced at a couple who'd been sitting in the last row but found only the man leaning back, arms spread across the adjacent seats, grinning. (His girlfriend must've gone to the bathroom.) Why did he look so happy? His eyes were closed, so he couldn't have been smiling at the film. I didn't fully understand why at the time, but I envied that man his bliss.

★★★

"What's your goal?" Frank asked.

"What do you mean?"

"What do you want to do with her?"

"Well . . ."

"Be careful, you're still underage."

"It's embarrassing . . ."

"You want to kiss her."

"Well . . . Yeah."

"I don't blame you. She's cute."

"Yes, she is."

"Have you ever kissed a girl?"

"What do you think?"

"It's no big deal."

"Not once you've done it."

"I promise, it's not a big deal. Just wait for the right moment and go for it."

"How will I know when it's the right moment?"

"She'll tell you."

"Really?"

"No, not really."

★★★

In all the films I'd seen, the man put his arm around the woman and pulled her close. The rest took care of itself. But based on her reaction to my earlier nudge, my arm was the last thing Cindy wanted wrapped around her. In fact, she was now leaning away from me, resting her elbow on the unshared armrest.

She's playing hard-to-get, I told myself. *This is a test of your courage. If you don't do something soon, she won't want to see you again.*

I inhaled deeply, turned to her, raised my arm slightly ... then lowered it and faced the screen. I couldn't do it.

Her father was late again. We stood in front of the theatre, several feet apart, avoiding each other's gaze. Our silence was drowned by happy couples streaming in and out of the theatre, laughing, holding hands, discussing the films they'd just seen or were about to see.

QUESTIONS: 1. Did Cindy want me to make a move?
2. If she did, and I kissed her, where would we be now? Happy. Laughing, probably. Talking, at least.
3. If she didn't want me to make a move, and I did anyway, where would we be?

"He's late," Cindy mumbled. She looked at her watch and sighed.

I asked her how she liked the movie.

"S'okay."

"What was your favourite part?"

"Uh ..."

"Favourite scene?"

"I don't know. What was yours?"

"Uh, I'm not sure. I guess I kinda liked them all."

It's never too soon to start lying to your soul-mate.

She looked away. "My father won't let me date. He thinks I'm too young."

"Oh."

I wanted to say a hundred things at once, but I could only bring myself to stare at her pink shoes.

Wait! But that meant her ambivalence had nothing to do with me. Her father was the problem. When I nudged her shoulder, her shock wasn't fear but sober protest. Secretly, desperately, hopelessly, she wanted me to grab her and show her what it means to be a woman. It must have taken all her strength not to collapse to the floor when I gave her that poem, or weep when I offered her snacks and a straw of her own. Instead, she simply sighed or rolled her eyes, each gesture hinting at the despair that she so courageously tried to conceal.

In the two and a half hours we spent together, she allowed herself one indulgence: she laughed at my joke in the car. She let herself embrace one moment of unrestrained happiness and hoped that it would be enough to sustain her in years to come, when all she would have are rose-tinted memories and a faded picture in a high-school yearbook.

Experiment 5: Happily Ever After

Plan A: Defeat the Insufferable Patriarch

Procedure:
1. On the drive home, batter away mundane questions like "How was the movie?" with a rhetorical jab like "Your daughter is fifteen years old. She can make her own decisions."
2. When inside her house, continue the conversation in the living room. (The kitchen contains too many sharp objects.) .
3. She will give a passionate defence of our love. Her father will grab her by the arms and try to shake sense into her, but I'll jump between them, fists on hips, chest puffed out, very gorilla-like. I'll say, "Stand aside, villain," like in films about forbidden romance. (Or was it "stand down"? They always demand that the villain stand somewhere ...)

Amendment: Maybe I am being unfair: her father is not exactly a villain. Despite his repressive parenting skills, he probably has good intentions. "Stand aside, old man!" might be more reasonable. Old people, especially old parents, have no understanding of love. Perhaps I should pity her father. He could never feel what I feel.

VARIABLE:	He still refuses to let me date Cindy.

Plan B: Running Away Together

PROCEDURE:	1. Find survival tools. [8]
	2. Ask Frank for advice.
	3. Ask parents for money.
	4. Ask parents to relocate. [9]

Cindy and I climbed in the car, but as soon as the doors closed I forgot what I'd wanted to say.

"How was the movie?" her father asked.

"Okay," Cindy replied. Her father looked at me in the mirror, smiling.

Not the right time, I told myself. *Keep quiet.*

He turned on the radio, and we spent the rest of the ride listening to songs about courage and heartbreak.

We pulled into Cindy's driveway. Her house was different than I'd imagined.

The insufferable patriarch met my gaze in the mirror. "You're just down the street, aren't you, Jeff?"

"Yeah, I am."

"Would you mind walking? The tank's a bit low."

"No, that's okay."

Her father rolled his eyes when I offered to walk his daughter to the door, but Cindy wore her usual mask of melancholy. She knew this was the end, at least until her knight-in-shining-armour could save her from her father. As we approached the house, side by side, I wanted to take her hand and whisper, as though she were fatally ill, "We're going to get through this."

---

[8] We would probably be in the woods for the first week or so, but once the police had given up on their search, we could live more freely in motels and camp sites.

[9] Cindy and I shouldn't have to live in squalor. She could stay with the family, and when we turned eighteen, we could get married and start our perfect life together.

Her father opened the door and entered. He turned to his daughter. "Cindy? Are you coming in?" She took a step forward, and I grabbed her hand.

"Just a second," I said.

Her father sighed and walked away. I peered into the foyer and caught a glimpse of the living room: my future battlefield.

"What is it?" she asked.

"Oh, nothing . . ." I reached behind her and pulled the door shut. (I hadn't pictured it being open in my image of our first kiss.) Still holding her hand, I drew the other one away from her side and held them together.

"I should really get going," she said, clearly uncomfortable.

I leaned forward and kissed her.

Clouds didn't part, planets didn't align, but for three endless seconds words like wet, scent, skin, and breath took on new meaning. I could feel her lips extend into a smile. They didn't kiss back, nor did they retreat. They simply waited for mine to detach.

When I finally pulled away, her smile was still intact. She was looking at her feet, and her cheeks were two shades redder.

"I should probably get going," she whispered.

"I'll call you." [10]

"That's okay," she replied. "I'll call you."

Some people go their whole lives without hearing sweeter sounds than these. She was so beguiled that she couldn't even muster the patience to wait for my call. I had made romantic history: *she* was going to call *me*.

I ran home, burst through the door, and rushed to the phone.

Frank was sitting at the kitchen table, eating Cheerios.

"How'd the date go?" he asked, chewing (as usual) with his mouth open, chomping each grain into submission.

"Great," I replied, ignoring his sadistic grin. The screen on the phone displayed its standard message: *No missed calls.*

"Did you kiss her?"

---

[10] Every "parting of lovers" scene ended with the man telling the woman he'd call her.

"She kissed me."

"Heyyyy," he said, raising the bowl in salute. "Very nice." He closed his eyes and tilted it back, slurping the milk. "Did you talk about yourself, like I suggested?"

"Yeah," I said, emphatically, feeling no obligation to be honest.

"Did you pick any fights?"

"Of course."

"Did you stare at her tits?"

"I'm not an idiot."

"Is that a yes or a no?"

"It's a yes, moron."

"Three seconds or less?"

"More."

He laughed. "Did you touch them?"

I looked down at the phone, wrapping the cord around my finger. It felt like a second skin, a kind of rubber armour.

"That's okay," he said, standing up. "You'll get 'em next time."

He walked to the sink. I wanted to knock the bowl out of his hand and strangle him with the phone cord.

"Who paid?" he asked, rinsing off his spoon. "You or her?"

I felt my eyes widen and my pulse increase.

"Oh," he mumbled, shaking his head. "Bad call."

He dried his hands and walked out of the kitchen. I could hear his footsteps march up the stairs and move across the ceiling.

When his bedroom door closed, I resumed my staring contest with the phone.

Don't panic, I told myself. *He's just trying to freak you out.*

I started pacing, checking the phone every few seconds to see if a new message—a more uplifting message—had somehow replaced *No missed calls*. I knew what I would find, yet each time I checked I felt the same flutter of hope, followed by the same punch of disappointment.

After a while, I decided to rest my feet.

I waited by the phone for nearly ten minutes before I realized that I hadn't even given her my number.

I leapt out of my chair and dialled her digits, only to hear endless ringing. One by one, the rose-coloured scenes in my head shattered. Was her father really the problem, or was her ambivalence truly meant for me?

Of course not. She loves me. She has to love me. Why else would she laugh at my joke in the car?

But when I replayed her adorable laugh in my mind, it became shrill and menacing, then faded to a sound worse than the silence we shared so often: the monotonous ringing of her telephone.

Just as I was about to hang up—and give up on Cindy once and for all—I realized that she'd probably found my number in the phone book and was trying to call me just as I was trying to call her. [11]

I would never doubt Cindy again. Together we would overcome all obstacles, all circumstances. I felt I could take on God, chance, fate—whatever the world could throw at me. There was only one person who could stand in the way of my happiness, and I trusted her completely, as all true lovers should.

I hung up the phone and sat tall in my chair, waiting for Cindy to call.

---

[11] This kind of miscommunication occurred in a half-dozen films I'd seen.

Tickle My Ear

MAX JR. & MEL

The bed squeaks. Max grunts. Mel moans.

"Tickle my ear," Max whispers.

"What?"

"Tickle my ear."

She tries to obey.

"No, don't flick it," he says. "Tickle it."

She softens her touch, massaging instead of stroking. "Like this?"

"Yeah." He closes his eyes and exhales in her face. His coffee breath makes her lightheaded. "Harder."

Her nails scrape his skin.

"Too hard," he says, pulling away. "You're scratching."

"Sorry." She makes adjustments, finding the middle-ground between nails and nothing.

"Ooooooh yeah," he moans. "That's it."

MAX SR. & RUTH

Ruth is on the couch in her bathrobe, watching an old home movie of a camping trip.

The living room is blandly decorated, colourless and bare. Even the furniture looks exhausted. Pale light pours in through the windows, soaking the room in a ghostly glaze.

Ruth sips her tea without taking her eyes off the screen. A young boy with a slingshot approaches the camera, running from something.

Mommy, he says. *Daddy's being mean.*

That's nice, Sweetie.

Mommy, he repeats, hiding behind a tree. *When I grow up, I wanna be like you.*

That's nice, Sweetie.

A key forces its way into the lock on the front door. Ruth sighs and closes her eyes, preparing for something she has faced a thousand times and would rather not face again.

A balding man in a suit enters the apartment, slamming the door behind him. He throws his coat, briefcase, and keys on the kitchen counter and opens the fridge.

Ruth does not bother to look. She has looked enough times to know what she will see. Her ears can set the scene, tell the story. She hears the clink of bottles, the crinkle of aluminum foil, the dull thuds of shifting cartons, half-filled with expired milk.

"Fuck," the man says, from inside the fridge. He slams the door, then stomps down the hall and enters the bedroom. Ruth hears him scream three times into a pillow and punch something hard.

"FUUUUUCK!"

Ruth mutes the TV.

The man returns, clutching his hand.

"You're supposed to punch the pillow, not the wall."

He pulls an ice tray out of the freezer, dumps the cubes on the counter, and tries to place them on his knuckles. They scatter as he touches them, sliding off the counter and onto the floor.

"Godmotherfuckingdammit . . ."

Ruth watches him, grinning as she sips her tea. More cubes slip off the counter.

"Sonofacocksuckingdonkey—"

"Maxy?"

"WHAT?"

"Have you considered using a towel?"

"NO!"

He grabs a towel from the cabinet and wraps the remaining ice in a bundle. He ties it around his hand and leans on the counter.

"Feel better?" Ruth asks, wearing a comfortable smile.

Max hangs his head.

"You're home pretty early."

Max lets out a sigh.

"Rough day at work?"

He tries to stand but slips on the ice and nearly collapses. "GODFUCKSLUT!"

Ruth raises the cup to her lips. "Mine was okay, thanks."

Max recovers and opens a cabinet under the sink. "Shit."

"What?"

"We're out of beer."

He slams the cabinet door and opens another above the sink. He takes out a bottle of whiskey, pours a large glass, and drinks half of it in a single gulp. He starts to pace in the living room, walking back and forth in front of the TV, forcing Ruth to tilt her head every few seconds.

"You won't believe what that asshole did today. That little shit. You won't believe what he made me—what he *wanted* me to do. I didn't do it, don't worry. I told the prick I'd never do it. I told him some people still have dignity. Some people can't be bought. I told him there's a line I don't cross." He takes a drink. "You know what that little shit said? He said, 'Don't say anything you can't take back. Take till the end of the day to decide.' Can you believe this fucking guy? I told him I didn't take things back, I mean the things I say, and unlike some other assholes I could mention, I don't bullshit people." He finishes his whiskey in one clean chug. "I told that little prick I don't put up with this shit. Not from him. Not from anyone. Even if it means getting fired, I don't care. I'd take my dignity over a pay check any day of the fucking week. 'Fucking fire me,' I said, 'or stop wasting my time.'" Max stops pacing and looks at Ruth. "Honey?"

Ruth continues to stare at the TV. The boy on-screen has wrapped his arms around the person holding the camera. A younger version of Max approaches, one with enough hair to form a respectable comb-over.

"Ruth."

"What?"

"Have you been listening?"

Without meeting his gaze, Ruth waves a dismissive hand and says, "Just do what he wants."

"Just do what he wants?" He glares at her, expecting her to glare back. "And you'd be okay with that? You'd be fine living with a man like that?"

"Like what?"

"Stop fucking around. A man without . . ."

"Testicles?"

"Dignity."

"Better than living with a man without a job."

Before Max can respond, the TV emits a muted burst of laughter. He looks from the screen to his wife, then back to the screen. "Why are you watching . . . Is this the one when you left us in the woods?"

"I told you I didn't like camping."

"Yes, you did. Over and over."

"And yet you dragged me out there. Over and over."

"It was good for Junior. He learned a few things."

"He certainly did."

Max looks down at his empty glass. He turns to the sink, overflowing with dirty plates and cutlery. "Where is he? He's supposed to do the dishes."

"I think he went to Mel's."

"That kid needs to get laid."

"Which one?"

"Which one do you think?"

Max Jr. & Mel

As they catch their breath, they hold the covers past their chest, staring wide-eyed at the ceiling. For the first time in years, Mel notices the glow-in-the-dark stars looking down at her. They are barely visible, thanks to the flat afternoon light, but their edges cast shadows.

She wonders if Max notices them too, and, if so, whether she should say something. No, that would probably just make things worse. He probably hasn't noticed. And even if he has, he probably doesn't care. He's probably too distracted by his own shame to detect or acknowledge anyone else's. (The key word in situations like these is "probably.")

Then again, why should she care if he sees them? Who is he to judge her, especially after what just happened? She shouldn't have to justify her decor—or anything else for that matter. So what if there are pieces of glow-in-the-dark plastic taped to her ceiling? She knows drug dealers who still sleep with their teddy bears.

Besides, her dad had installed the stars more than eleven years ago, when her main goals in life involved ponies and a trip to Disneyland. Six-Year-Old Mel liked them at first, but their novelty soon wore off, and they became part of the landscape—invisible during the day, invisible at night. Over the years, as her toys were replaced by clothes, the majority of her childhood relics were hidden in boxes and moved to the basement. They're to be uncovered, she assumes, when they're old enough to trigger nostalgia instead of shame.

Without tilting her head, Mel scans the room for embarrassing items. Nothing stands out. Her walls are bare; her desk is tidy; her books are shelved. Even Max pointed out, during a previous visit, that her furniture and decorations seemed somewhat conservative for someone so liberal. The drapes match the dresser. The dresser matches the bed. The bed matches the carpet. (Which also matches the drapes.)

She feels safe, scandal-free, until she spots her diary on the desk, opened to yesterday's entry. Shit, shit, shit. Her eyes dart back and forth across the ceiling, bouncing from star to star in search of a solution.

If Max reads it, she thinks, he'll never speak to me again. I have to hide it. I have to burn it. I have to get up and throw it out the window.

Normally, she has enough foresight to put things away, but today they rushed upstairs before she had a chance to hide it in her drawer.

She knows what it says, word-for-word:

Monday, April the fucking 10th.

I can never tell what Max is thinking. What he wants from life. What he wants from me. After all the talks, the texts, and the make-out sessions, I still don't know where we are or what we are. I wish he could just be honest, for once. I don't care about his family or his stupid insecurities. I don't even care about The Ear Bandage Rumor. (Which is bullshit, anyway. Max is dumb, but he's not that dumb.) I just want to know if he's serious, if he wants my mind as well as my body.

And even if he only wants my body, that's fine. I just want him to tell me. I swear to God, he's such a guy sometimes. He thinks that bragging and teasing and hiding his emotions is the only way to get laid. That might work for club girls, for drunk chicks who scream YOLO, but it doesn't work for me, let alone 90 percent of girls/women. He must have learned this Be A Man thing from his dad. (Not to mention his macho classmates. And patriarchal gender roles. And almost every facet of mainstream culture that reinforces them.)

But he's one of the good ones, relatively speaking. He's no feminist, but at least he's well-intentioned. At least he gives a shit. When he fucks up, he admits it and tries to do better. That's more than I can say for most of his male counterparts . . .

In any case, I think my virgin status freaked him out, and now he's afraid to make a move. Ever since I told him, he's been overcompensating, trying to impress me. I thought telling him the truth would help him relax. I'm a beginner too, and I just want my first time to be nice. It doesn't have to be amazing. Shit, chances are, it'll suck. But at least I'll have a nice guy to share it with.

He better make a move tomorrow. I would if I could, but I can't. Girls aren't allowed. It's like ballroom dancing. Guys still lead; girls still follow. Hopefully, that'll change someday, but that day ain't today, or tomorrow, or any day in the foreseeable future.

You know what? Fuck it. When he comes over tomorrow, I'll just grab him by the dick and pull him into my room.

She imagines Max's face when he reads it. She imagines what he'll say, how he'll say it, and what she'll say after he says it. She imagines a three-act fight that she knows will never take place. Not because she'd stop him, but because Max wouldn't read her diary if it were opened to a drawing of her breasts and placed on his nose. He respects her right to privacy almost as passionately as he protects his right to ignorance.

Mel inhales deeply and slowly, trying to mask her moment of panic. Her chest moves, but nothing else. Her breath is soundless, a stream of anxiety flowing out and away.

Max, on the other hand, is still panting, despite his efforts to cease. Fair enough, she thinks. He's not exactly an athlete, and he did most of the work. Three and a half minutes of work, but work nonetheless. She shouldn't have tickled his ear. That's what put him over the top.

Suddenly calm and secure, she imagines what she might write for today's entry, after Max has left. She goes through drafts on the ceiling: scribbling, erasing, refining.

After numerous rewrites and revisions, she settles on the following:

Tuesday, April the goddamn 11th.

Losing your virginity is not what it used to be. At least that's what people keep telling me. Old people, mostly. People who lost their virginity in the early 1920s. Like Mom and Dad.

Bullshit. It's exactly what it used to be. Just as awkward, just as traumatic. But no one wants to admit it. Our parents and our parents' parents (and probably their parents) would like us to believe that sex— along with everything else—was better in their day. More noble, more elegant, more efficient. Before the age of dildos and vibrators, when virginity and marriage went hand-in-hand, sex meant something. It was beautiful and poetic and life-changing.

Bullshit, I say again. Bullshit. Each generation is as clumsy as the last, as clueless as the next. And Max, the poor, deluded fellow, is no exception. [frowny face]

P.S. Maybe the rumour's true. Maybe he tried to tickle her lobe and poked her drum by accident. (Maybe.)

Max finally breaks the silence: "Sorry, could you pass my glasses?"

"Oh. Sure."

She reaches for their thick, black glasses on the bedside table. She hands Max his and puts on her own.

Max looks under the covers, then at Mel. "What should I do with the . . ."

She furrows her brow, confused.

He nods to his crotch.

"Oh." She plucks a tissue from her bedside table and hands it to him.

"Thanks," he says, reaching under the covers. He takes off his condom, wraps it in the tissue, and places it beside the bed. He notices something dark on the tips of his fingers. "Can I grab another? There's some blood on my hands."

"Oh. Sure." She hands him a couple of tissues, then looks under the covers, self-consciously. "Should've used a towel or something."

"It's okay. It'll wash out."

"Yeah."

They stare at the ceiling, hoping the other will make the first move.

Suddenly, Max says, "Sorry about all the hair, by the way."

"Hmm?"

"The hair." He points. "I didn't get a chance to trim."

"Oh, that's okay."

"I wasn't expecting to . . . you know . . ."

"That's all right. I wasn't either."

"But you're glad you did?"

"Of course. And I'm glad it was with you instead of . . . some jerk."

"Me too."

They trade smiles and look away.

"Just for the record," Max says, "you're looking good down there. Hair-wise."

"Oh. Thanks."

"It's well-landscaped."

She grins. "Well-landscaped, you say?"

"Well-landscaped, well-groomed, well-crafted. You have sublime shrubbery."

She laughs.

"A bodacious bush."

She laughs harder.

"It smells nice too."

She stops laughing. "What?"

"Is that not a compliment? I thought it was a compliment."

"It's a weird compliment."

"But it's true. You have a nice-smelling . . . lady part."

"You can't even say vagina?"

"A nice-smelling vagina. There."

" 'Nice-smelling' . . ."

"Yeah. Like sushi or something."

"Sushi?! Sushi doesn't smell good!"

"I love the smell of sushi."

Mel lets out a sigh of frustration.

"What? It's not a bad smell. It's not like . . . sewer fish, or roasted—"

"Sewer fish?"

"It's a nice smell!"

"What the fuck is a sewer fish?"

"You know, one of those radioactive . . . the one on The Simpsons. Or Spider-Man." He scratches his head and squints at the ceiling. "I think there was a sewer fish in Spider-Man—"

"There's no such thing as sewer fish."

"Okay. A) Yes, there is. B) I was just trying to give you a compliment."

"A creepy compliment."

"Still a compliment."

She scoffs.

He turns away, crossing his arms into the sheet and pulling it tighter.

She stares at his back, spotted with pimples and patches of hair. She takes a deep breath. "Sorry."

His back doesn't budge.

She reaches for his shoulder, half-covered by the pink of her sheets. "Hey. I'm sorry." When her fingers find their target, it twitches, and her fingers retreat.

Max Sr. & Ruth

Ruth is still on the couch, watching the home movie. She spots a fly on the wall above the TV screen. The wall's only decoration, the room's only patch of life. The kitchen and bedrooms are no less bare, no more inviting. They have lived here for nearly a year, but they only unpacked the essentials. No posters, no pictures, no star-spangled ceilings. They don't want this place—this "cave with no leg room," as Ruth calls it—to feel like home, because it isn't and never will be. In fact, two of its three tenants are planning to move. One, to college; the other, as far from the third as humanly possible. Even the third had moved in expecting to leave (though not in the same sense as the others) and refused to fully unpack. As a result, the apartment feels anonymous, like a hotel room that spends most of its time waiting for visitors. Maids go in and out, dusting tables, fluffing pillows, but no one lingers if they can help it. Eleven-hundred square feet devoid of anything human, filled to the brim with nothing in particular. Like a shopping mall. Or an unmarked grave.

Ruth looks over at her husband, pouring another whiskey, and wonders how much longer she can tolerate this charade. Junior is about to graduate—thank God—but he won't be moving out until he starts college in the fall. Which leaves five months, give or take, of imprisonment.

Unlike most spouses, Ruth doesn't wonder how her marriage unraveled. She knows. She could write a book about it. *Ten Simple Steps to an Awful Marriage. Five Easy Ways to Ruin Your Life.* And unlike most spouses, she didn't watch her partner become a stranger or morph into a monster. She saw the monster on their very first date, when he grabbed her butt in the park. And on the second, when he grabbed her breast. And on the third, fourth, and fifth, when he grabbed everything else. On the sixth, she learned that the monster didn't like condoms, and by the seventh, she had unwrapped the monster's present: A present that could not be exchanged or returned and would cost eighteen years of her life.

She knows what her husband thinks but doesn't have the courage to say. She knows that, behind his macho veneer of indifference, he's wondering what happened to his beloved Ruthie. When they started dating, she was fun and alive and exciting. In a word, happy. (Wrong.) Then Junior came along, and everything changed. (Wrong.) She became uptight and moody. (Wrong.) When they started dating, she never disagreed with her beloved Maxy. (Wrong.) But these days, a fight-free day was a rarity, not to mention a blessing. (Less wrong.) And he honestly doesn't know why. (Right.)

Correction Number One: She wasn't happy. She was somewhat content for a month or so, until he knocked her up and convinced her, for propriety's sake, to marry him.

Correction Number Two: Nothing changed when Junior came along. Ruth was still Ruth and always would be. She simply developed a new set of goals and priorities, none of which included her husband.

Correction Number Three: She did not become uptight and moody. She had always been uptight and moody. She just stopped caring if anyone noticed.

Correction Number Four: She *always* disagreed with her beloved Maxy. She just didn't bother to tell him.

Max is right, however, on a couple of points: Ruth was, is, and always will be fun, as well as alive and exciting—just not around him. She has lots of vitality saved up; she simply refuses to spend it on inferior products.

Max is also right, to a certain extent, about Junior. When Ruth became pregnant, she considered having an abortion—in fact, she even made an appointment and drove to the clinic—but she couldn't bring herself to go through with it. She felt, rightly or wrongly, that things happened for a reason, and that she was meant to have this child, with this man. Whenever she found herself fantasizing about leaving Max, she thought of her father (from whom she had not heard in over thirty-five years) and reminded herself that a weak male presence was better than a strong male absence. She hoped, against all odds, that Max would teach his son to be a decent member of society—in other words, to be the Anti-Max—and, over the years, as her hopes diminished, she found herself frequently frustrated but rarely disappointed.

Two incomes were better than one, she told herself, and Junior deserved a proper family. Max, for all his limitations, was at least well-intentioned, not to mention loyal. "Like a golden retriever," her girlfriends said. "A golden retriever with anger problems." Ruth knew that her rationalizations were rationalizations, but she didn't care. She was determined to stay with Max until Junior left for college. Every few months, she'd pack a suitcase, get in the car, and drive until she no longer recognized the names on the signs, but after an hour or two, she'd calm down and remind herself why she was doing what she was doing. Like a recovering alcoholic counting days of sobriety, she carried Junior's class photos in her purse to mark her achievement and to help her stay focused. Each one meant another year of hardship overcome, another year closer to freedom. Not surprisingly, her girlfriends disapproved of her plan. Womanhood, to them, was about making choices, and although they never overtly disowned her, their interactions became less and less frequent, until Ruth stopped seeing them altogether. Her prison, she argued, was self-imposed. She *had* made a choice. It just wasn't the choice they wanted.

Ruth watches the young Junior stuff a burnt marshmallow into his mouth and lick his fingers. She turns up the volume when she sees him turn to his father.

Daddy, how do you get girls?

Uh oh, says Ruth, playfully, from behind the camera. *I think someone has a crush.*

The blonde or the redhead? asks Max, grinning his infamous grin.

They have names, you know.

Max ignores his wife's comment and wraps his arm around his son, pulling him closer. *You get girls*, he says, *by being a man.*

I am a man! his son exclaims, flexing his stringy biceps.

Max laughs and pats his back. *You're getting there. First, we need to put some meat on those bones. Toughen you up a bit.* He hands the boy a freshly burnt wiener and a stale bun. *Here. Have a hot dog.*

He's fine, Ruth says, *as he is.*

Max glares at the woman behind the camera.

Ruth looks over at the man behind the counter, pouring himself another drink. "What was the name of that lake called? Okachobee? Okachibee? "Oka" something . . ."

"Will you turn that shit off? I'm trying to have a conversation here."

"A conversation . . ." Ruth mutes the TV.

"You think I should give up. Just crawl into the office tomorrow with my tail between my legs—a tail where my dick used to be. Is that your position? I just want to be clear on this."

"He's going to fire you."

Max folds his arms and forces a condescending smile. "Thanks, hun. I can always count on you to cheer me up."

"That's what I'm here for."

He finishes his drink and starts pouring another. "So how was *your* day?"

"My day?"

"I told you about mine. It's only fair you tell me about yours."

"Fair . . ."

"You know what I mean."

"My day was fine."

"What did you do?"

"Not much."

"Did you send out those resumes?"

"Not yet."

"Did you hear back from anyone?"

"Not yet."

"Did you call anyone?"

"Not yet."

"Then what the hell did you do?"

"I went to the doctor."

"And that took the whole day?"

"No, that took the morning. In the afternoon, I went grocery shopping and cleaned the apartment. (Thanks for noticing.) I was going to send out resumes and make some calls, but I took a break to eat lunch and turned on the TV. Ten minutes later, you came home. Is that a satisfactory account of my activities?"

"You couldn't find time to drop off your resumes?"
"Nope."
"It takes five minutes. You walk to the fucking box and put them in the slot. I'm pretty sure you could manage it."

Ruth sips her tea.

"What did the doctor say?"
"Nothing good."
"What did he say?"
"He said I need more rest."
"More rest?! How's that possible? That's all you've been doing for six fucking months!"
"The stress is wearing me down."
"What stress?"
"The old stress. From work."
"You haven't been at work in—"
"Six months. I'm aware. I need more time."
"To do what exactly? Drop dead?"

She mimics his condescending smile. "Thanks, hun. I can always count on you to cheer me up."

"That's what I'm here for." He returns to the kitchen and gathers ingredients for a sandwich. Bread. Mayo. Cold cuts. Lettuce. "So what are you going to do then?"

"As in?"
"As in work. You have to go back to work."
"I'd rather not think about that right now."
"Well, I'm sorry, but you have to start thinking about it. Especially if that prick fires me."
"Don't get fired then."
"You're hilarious."
"I'm serious."

He slams the half-empty jar of mayo on the counter. "You can't just sit there and do nothing. You can't. I won't let you."

"Oh, you won't?"
"That's right. I won't."
"Well then . . ." She un-mutes the TV and starts watching.
"Where's your fucking self-respect?"
"It's hiding."

Someone on the TV squeals with joy.

"WILL YOU TURN THAT SHIT OFF."

Ruth turns up the volume.

Max bangs on the counter with his fist. "HEY!"

Ruth smiles at him.

"Fuck it," he says, pulling a knife out of the drawer. "I don't care."

"Yes, you do."

He puts down the knife and glares at her. "What was that?"

Ruth stares at him for a moment, expressionless, then turns back to the TV.

Max picks up the knife. "That's what I thought."

Max Jr. & Mel

Max has rotated 90 degrees, facing the star-spangled ceiling instead of her closet. He refuses to turn the full 180. That would mean facing Mel.

Besides, he has turned enough; the rest is her responsibility. He is literally meeting her halfway. If she refuses to take the bait and say something, the fault, as they say, is not in her stars but in herself. He memorized that line in 10th Grade English and cherished it ever since. In the face of biological determinism, free-will debunkers, Neo-Freudians, and over-controlling parents, the line has become a kind of motto. He refuses to blame his stars for his condition, whether good, bad, or somewhere in between. *He* is the master of his fate, the captain of his soul. That was the other line he committed to memory. Though he can never remember who said it.

Speaking of stars, Max wonders about the ceiling. He doesn't want to ask—especially now—but he has questions. In fact, he's tempted, if more insults come his way, to use her star-studded ceiling as fodder for comebacks. But he's hoping things won't come to that. Despite his wounded ego, he would like to make peace, not war. He just wants her to throw down the first rifle and wave the white flag.

To be honest, he can't blame her for feeling underwhelmed by his sexual prowess. He has never lied to her—and never will—but he has certainly embellished and equivocated. (How else is one supposed to get laid?) He has lied, however, to others, mostly about his sexual expertise, and mostly to people who know Mel, in hopes that the gossip machine will keep her informed.

If he mentions the stars, will that help break the tension or merely add insult to injury? They aren't *that* embarrassing. If anything, they're cute, but chances are if he says as much, the comment will find some way to offend her. (Like his well-intentioned—and, in hindsight, ill-advised—vagina-sushi comparison.) He'd love to know how the stars got there, why they are still there, and whether she has any plans to take them down. Granted, he kept his Star Wars curtains and Iron Man bedspread until he was thirteen, but Thirteen-Year-Old Max and Eighteen-Year-Old Max were two completely different beings. One masturbated three times a day; the other, five. One liked girls for their boobies; the other, for everything else. (Brain included.)

He wonders: Is she staring at the same stars? Is she linking one to another, forming constellations in her mind? Or is she preoccupied with something non-star-related? Maybe she's wondering what he's thinking. Or wondering if he's wondering what she's thinking. Maybe she's replaying her first sexual experience in her head, groan by groan, thrust by thrust—savoring, critiquing, repressing.

Max had described his first time to classmates as "epic" and "immensely satisfying for both parties," but, in reality, it was just as awkward and short-lived as 99 percent of all virginity losses. First, he had trouble putting on the condom, which sprung off the tip of his penis and hit the girl's nipple. Then, after forty-six seconds of clueless humping, he moaned—or, more accurately, shouted—in her ear and nearly caused permanent damage. Her doctor prescribed pills and covered the ear in a bandage, which she had to wear for over a month. Her official excuse was an infection, but a few days after the incident, her closest friends began to point and giggle whenever Max would walk by in the cafeteria. At this stage in his life, girls had many reasons to giggle at him, so he didn't jump to conclusions. But he couldn't deny that the timing was suspicious.

For weeks he wanted to apologize, but he couldn't bring himself to speak to her—or even look her in the eye—until the bandage came off. It was a constant reminder of his impotence, his shameful lack of masculinity. High school graduation was only a few months away, and—excluding hand jobs, blow jobs, and other job-like activities—he'd only had three sexual encounters, none of which gave him reasons to brag. (In fact, each one gave him new reasons to lie.)

Max decided to enhance his expertise by watching instructional sex videos online. He found it hard, however, to focus on the instructional aspects of the videos when the sex aspects were so captivating. In fact, he'd usually only last a few minutes before he felt compelled to put aside his notebook and retrieve the lotion and tissue box from the bathroom. When he finally realized how little he'd gained and how much he could potentially lose, he stopped browsing the internet for carnal advice. As far as he knew, Mom and Dad didn't monitor his search history, but they were bound to discover his research materials eventually.

So he went to the public library instead. He didn't have the courage to borrow books, but he glanced at them when the librarian wasn't looking. In a book on Kama Sutra, he learned (among other things) that the ear was an erogenous zone, and that licking, tickling, and massaging the ear could provide erotic pleasure. Intrigued and inspired, he put the book aside and marched into the bathroom to tickle his ears. He quickly realized, however, that it was impossible to tickle himself, so he tried massaging his ears instead. No reaction. He would need someone else's touch—preferably, someone with a vagina—so he vowed to ask the next girl with whom he hooked up to tickle, lick, and/or massage his ears.

That girl, for better or worse, turned out to be Mel, an old friend whom he had always liked but never enough to tell her. They had known each other for nearly a decade, and although they came close a few times, they never quite connected. What the hell, he thought, one day in biology, when he noticed Mel's new hair cut. She wasn't exactly a 10—or even an 8 or a 9—but neither was he. And that was okay. After four years of high school, he was tired of 9s and 10s. He had learned to reel in his expectations and settle for substance over shape. He wanted cute, not hot; the girl next door instead of the porn star. After all, his "dream girl" would probably be nothing like the girl of his dreams.

(His dad had always taught him to punch his weight. "10s date 10s," he said, "and 7s date 7s." He never assigned a number to Max, but Max guessed that 7 was not arbitrarily chosen. Nor was it entirely accurate. His father probably thought he was a 6—maybe even a 5—but he just didn't want to admit it. Max's mom, on the other hand, thought that anyone, regardless of rank, could date anyone. "You're living proof of that," she'd tell her husband, after calling his system a "pile of reductionist bullshit." "Bullshit that helps guys get girls," he'd reply, fully aware of how much she resented his theory that girls were something to "get," like DVDs and groceries. Max Sr. had a zero-sum approach to relationships: "Either you get girls," he'd say, "or girls get you.")

So, during the ten minute break between biology and calculus, Max asked her out. And weeks later, after hours of hand-holding, making-out, and exploratory petting, he found himself beguiled. Mel was supposed to be a placeholder, a chance to gain experience and build confidence. He had expected to like her, want her, maybe even admire her. But he hadn't expected to fall in love with her.

Yet here he is. And there she is. Side by side, refusing to talk.

"FYI . . ." she says, breaking the silence. "You have a nice . . . you know . . ."

"Hmm?"

"It's nice. It's . . . long . . . and straight."

He allows himself a laugh, barely audible.

"I'm serious," she says. "A lot of them are all crooked and curvy."

"How many have you seen?"

"Uh . . . Not too many. Not in person, at least."

He turns to her and scans her face, confused.

"Yours is nice," she continues. "It's not too veiny. And the top is nice and round. Like a helmet."

"What kind of helmet?"

"I don't know. Just a helmet. An army helmet."

Max does not seem satisfied.

"Some of them look angry, you know, like they're going to mug you or something . . . But yours looks happy."

"I have a very well-adjusted penis."

"I know you do." She kisses him on the cheek.

"You're pretty good, by the way. You know, for a beginner."

She scoffs. "I'm a pro. You're a beginner."

"I'll have you know, I've had four times as much sex as you've had."

"It shows."

He grins proudly, then as the ambiguity sinks in he furrows his brow, perplexed.

"Tell me, Casanova: were these four separate ladies or four separate incidents? Or four separate ladies *and* four separate incidents?"

Max tries to formulate an answer.

"Or fewer than four separate ladies and four separate incidents?"

Max sighs.

"Or four separate *men* and four separate incidents?"

"Okay. A) Gross. B) I object to the term 'incident.' It sounds suspicious."

"And are you referring to duration or to specific acts? Does your criteria differentiate between quality and quantity, and if so, how so, and if not, why not?"

"What?"

"Nothing, sweetie. I'm just messing with you."

"Oh." Max pulls the covers over his chest. "By the way, you left out four separate ladies and fewer than four separate incidents."

"That would imply a threesome. You haven't have a threesome."

"How do you know?"

"I've known you since you wet your pants at recess. You haven't had a threesome."

"A middle-aged couple online once asked me to take a well-oiled piece of—"

"Please, don't finish that sentence."

"They seemed nice to me."

"I'm sure they were lovely. Can we change the subject?"

"Sure. You brought it up."

She opens her mouth but resists the urge to respond.

Their eyes wander across the ceiling, searching for something to say.

Max turns to her, smiling. "Wanna go again?"

"Go where?" She interprets his grin. "Oh. No. No way."

He recoils, offended, and turns away. No middle-ground 90 this time. Full 180.

She reaches out to comfort him. "No, I just mean right now. Not right now. Later maybe."

"Fine."

"Thanks though. For offering."

Max Sr. & Ruth

Max continues working on his sandwich. Chop, chop, slice. Chop, chop, slice.

Ruth has set the TV at a reasonable volume. Max doesn't watch, but he listens. He recognizes the arguments, the lines of dialogue, recycled from countless fights before. In this scene, Junior has wandered off, leaving Max and Ruth alone to argue about everything from tent-building techniques to parenting ideologies. Ruth impales a tent pole in the ground and walks off into the trees. Max yells something obscene, but she keeps walking.

Ruth is clearly trying to tell him something by watching this video. But Max doesn't care. If she has something to say, she can man-up and say it to his face. This passive aggressive shit doesn't work on him. She knows that. And she knows that he knows that she knows that. And yet she does it anyway. Because she knows that it *does* work, on some level, in some way. And she knows that he knows that she knows that.

What he doesn't know is why she's so hard on him. And so soft on Junior. And so hard on him for not being soft on Junior. Soft helps no one. (He has explained this many times.) Hard is a necessary evil, a required course called Growing Up 101. Max sensed early on that his son was a bit girly—"sensitive," as Ruth called it—but he refused to let her convince Junior that it was okay to be weak.

He needed, as a father, to teach his son the truth about girls and women: "If you work hard and do the right things, girls will come. But you have to be ready. Girls don't want some scrawny little wimp. They want men." When Ruth heard Max say this, just months after the camping trip, she nearly dropped a dish on the kitchen floor. "Girls," she explained, "aren't trophies you get if you do your homework. They're not things to earn. They're people." Then Max said something about respect and how it's earned, not given, and that nothing in life is free. "Love is free," she said, taking her son's hand. Max scoffed and pulled him away from his mother. "Don't listen to that sensitive crap," he said, walking Junior to his room.

To this day, Max has no idea how Ruth really feels about him. From Date One, he was head-over-heels and just assumed that his feelings were mutual. If he wondered, from time to time, why his wife seemed to hate everything he did, said, and thought, he would blame the birth of Junior and the loss of his job—both results of sexual misconduct. Junior, the unlucky accident, was a walking condom commercial. His high-powered job, on the other hand, evaporated when a co-worker filed a sexual harassment complaint, claiming that Max had grabbed her "caboose." (His term, not hers.) Naturally, he dismissed the allegation as unfounded, motivated by petty office politics; however, a few days later, six more women came forward, complaining of similar behavior. Groping in the break room. Winking as he passed their desks. Flirting at social functions. Talking too close. Touching. Brushing. Staring. Some had text messages to prove their claims; others had emails and security camera footage. By Friday, the jury was in, and Max was out. Ruth stood by him—in public and private—pretending to believe every word of his alibis, but she knew. And he knew that she knew. But neither would ever admit it.

After Max was fired, they were forced to sell their two-storey house and move into a two-bedroom apartment. (Their house had been lavish, comfortable to a fault, as intoxicating as it was unaffordable.) Eventually, Ruth lost her job, due to the flailing economy, and Max found work—after months of fruitless searching—as a clerk. He hadn't worked such a menial job since his first years out of business school, but with his new reputation as a sexual predator, he was lucky to find anything. He went from a corner office with a view of the park to a cubicle beside the men's washroom. His salary dropped from six digits to five. He went from commanding respect to inspiring gossip, and instead of firing people for the hell of it, he spent most of his days fighting to stay employed. Each evening, he would come home with a new list of whiskey-fueled complaints. Bill did this. Sandra said that. Sandra did this while Bill said that. After a while, he began to sound like Junior, returning from a rough day at school. But Ruth didn't mind. In fact, she seemed to enjoy his complaints.

The source of Ruth's resentment wasn't Junior or the new apartment or Max's workplace indiscretions. It was Max. A simple fact that he could neither accept nor fully understand. And Ruth liked it that way. He lived in a state of perpetual ignorance—towards the world, towards his family, towards himself—and, from Ruth's point-of-view, it was only fair that he die in it.

Hi, Daddy.

Max looks up from the cutting board. The volume on the TV has increased.

Where's Mommy? asks the same small voice, stepping out of the trees.

Gone.

The camera has been left on a rock, pointed at the campfire. A thin trail of smoke rises from the black, ash-ridden wood, whose embers continue to glow and fade, gasping for breath. The flame, a mere flicker of its former size, struggles to stay lit.

Where did she go? Junior asks, scanning his surroundings.

She'll be back, Maxy. Don't worry. He enters the frame and hugs his son. *She has nowhere else to go.*

"When's Junior coming home?" asks Max.

"You know, he looked like me back then," Ruth mumbles. "The eyes . . . cheekbones . . ."

"When's he coming home?"

"But now he looks like you."

Ruth mutes the TV and studies Max as he makes his sandwich, calculating her next move. She suddenly assumes a cheerful, high-energy persona. "What are ya makin' there?"

"What do you care?"

"I'm just curious."

"A sandwich."

"What kind?"

"Roast beef."

"Ah."

Max sighs impatiently. "You want one?"

"No, thank you."

"You sure?"

"How about a salad?"

"You don't want roast beef?"

"I feel more like a salad."

"A salad . . ."

"Hope you don't mind."

"No," Max mumbles, "it's fine." He opens the fridge and searches for ingredients.

Ruth watches him, grinning. "You sure you don't mind?"

"No. It's just . . ."

"What?"

"It just takes more work, that's all."

"More work? Maxy, my darling, it takes five minutes. You just chop some lettuce, chop some celery, chop some carrots—"

"I don't have carrots."

"You don't have carrots?"

Another sigh. "I don't have carrots."

"Well, what do you have then?"

"Broccoli."

"Broccoli . . ."

"You still want the salad?"

"Yeah, why not."

Max starts washing the ingredients in the sink.

"Would've been better with carrots though . . ."

Max turns off the water. "What?"

"Nothing, Maxy. Just thinking out loud."

Max starts chopping the celery and the lettuce. "What were you thinking?"

"Oh, just about carrots. How they really make a salad worth eating."

Max begins chopping in quick slashing motions.

"Everything else is nice. Lettuce. Celery. Broccoli. But at the end of the day . . ."

Max stabs the vegetables into a pile of colourful flakes.

" . . . carrots are the only ones that matter."

Max cuts his finger. "FUCK!" He slams the knife on the counter, rushes to the bathroom, and turns on the tap.

"What happened, Maxy?"

"What do you think?" he yells. "I cut myself!"

"What?"

Max marches into the living room, dripping wet.

"I said, 'I cut myself chopping *your* fucking salad!'"

He returns to the bathroom.

"All right," Ruth says, smiling. "Take it easy. It's not like it's *my* fault."

"What?"

"It's not my fault."

Max turns off the tap and returns to the living room with a bandage. "What?"

"I said, 'I'm sorry about your finger.'"

"Oh. Don't worry. It's not your fault." Max picks up the knife and cleans it off in the sink.

Ruth gets up and walks into the kitchen. She takes the knife gently out of his hand and holds it, staring into his eyes. Max looks confused and scared, despite his attempts to hide his fear. She smiles and lays the knife on the counter.

"I'll tell you what." She leads him by the shoulders to the couch. "You just relax, and I'll bring you your sandwich."

"You don't have to do that—"

"It's what I'm here for."

She returns to the kitchen.

"Uh . . . thanks, hun."

"It's the least I can do."

He sighs, letting his head fall back against the wall. "I love you, Ruthie. You know that, don't you?"

"I know."

"Even if I get upset sometimes . . . It's got nothing to do with you."

"I know, Maxy. I know."

"Do you love me?"

"I'm surprised you have to ask."

Ruth stabs the sandwich with toothpicks, then cuts it in half and puts it on a plate. She summons the poise of a ballerina and the smile of a stripper as she brings the sandwich to Max.

"Thanks," he says. "You're a doll."

Max Jr. & Mel

After a brief period of absentminded star-gazing, during which he finds Orion's Belt beside an oddly-shaped Little Dipper, Max asks Mel, "Does this mean we're dating?"

She furrows her brow. "Aren't we already dating?"

"We've been hooking up. I wouldn't call that dating."

"We haven't been hooking up. Hooking up is sex."

"Hooking up is any sex-related activity involving two or more parties. I googled it."

"We've been seeing each other."

"Okay. A) How do you define seeing? And B) No, we haven't."

"Okay. A) You're a nerd. B) You're a nerd. C) I won't answer that. And D) You're a nerd."

"So does that mean we're dating?"

"Yes, moron. That means we're dating."

"I thought we were 'seeing each other'."

"I'm going to bite your dick off."

Max grins, staring up at the star-studded ceiling. "Is this how you always imagined your first time?"

"Yes," she says sarcastically. "This is exactly how I imagined my first time. Right down to the . . ."

"What?"

"No, never mind."

"What?"

"It doesn't matter."

"Come on. I'm curious."

"It's nothing. Don't worry about it."

He scans her face for clues. "Are you screwing with me?"

"Yes," she replies, turning away, "I'm screwing with you."

His grin fades. "Holy shit. You're not screwing with me."

She massages her temple.

"Please tell me you're screwing with me."

"I'm screwing with you."

"Oh God." He looks up at the ceiling, this time ignoring the stars. "What did I do?"

"What?"

"I thought you were happy. You looked like you were happy. You *sounded* like you were happy—"

"Happy with what?"

"WITH MY PERFORMANCE."

Mel starts laughing.

"Stop laughing at me."

"I'm not laughing at you."

She keeps laughing.

"It seems like you're laughing at me."

"I'm not, I swear. It's just . . . your 'performance'"?

"So I didn't do anything wrong."

"No, you were fine."

"You were totally satisfied."

"Well . . ."

He glares at her. "Well, what?"

"I don't know about totally satisfied. I mean, are we ever totally satisfied?"

"I was!"

"I know *you* were. God, the neighbours know *you* were."

"They probably think I was alone."

"Stop it. You were fine."

"Just fine?"

"You know what I mean. You were good."

"Good?"

"It was awesome, okay? It was a religious experience. I finally know the meaning of life."

"Okay. Jesus."

"He was there too. And Joseph. And two of the wise men. The third guy couldn't make it."

"I get the picture."

"Great."

He folds his arms. "So what was it exactly?"

She groans.

"I think I have a right to know."

"It wasn't anything in particular."

"Was it anything in general?"

"It wasn't anything at all. I can't even believe we're having this conversation."

"Well, if you would just tell me, we could stop having this convers—"

"TICKLE MY EAR! TICKLE MY EAR! WHAT THE FUCK IS TICKLE MY EAR?!"

Max is stunned.

"Who says that? God!" She turns away completely, pulling the sheet tight across her chest.

"For the record," Max mutters, "the ear is a well-known erogenous zone."

"Well-known to whom exactly?"

"The people . . . who know . . . about erogeny."

"It's well-known to sewer fish."

"Those exist, by the way."

"Why are you awake? Aren't men supposed to fall asleep after sex?"

"I had a latte. Caffeine keeps me up."

Mel exhales deeply, half-frustrated, half-fatigued.

They stare at the ceiling. Both notice the stars. Neither care.

"Now what?" asks Mel, after a long silence.

Max turns to her, smiling. "Wanna go again?"

Mel turns to him, expressionless.

Max Sr. & Ruth

Max struggles to eat his sandwich with damaged hands: the left from the knife, the right from the wall. He takes slow, lethargic bites. Ruth chews her salad noisily, using her whole jaw to crush the celery between her teeth.

After she swallows, she asks, "How is it?"

"Good. Really good. Thanks, hun."

"I'm glad you like it."

"How's your salad?"

"Perfect. Thanks for asking."

"I'm sorry about earlier . . ."

"That's okay."

"It's no way for a man to act."

"Hey, Maxy?"

"Yeah."

"Would you mind doing me a favour?"

"Anything, Ruthie. What is it?"

"Would you mind running down to the post office to drop off my resumes?"

"Uh . . ."

"The doctor said I shouldn't strain myself."

"Oh. Okay."

"I shouldn't walk unless I have to."

"It's okay, Ruthie. I'm happy to do it."

"Thanks, hun."

"Is there anything else I can do?"

"No, nothing right now. Thanks for asking though."

"Anytime, Ruthie. That's what I'm here for."

Ruth suddenly stands and takes off her bathrobe, revealing the nightgown underneath. "Maxy . . ."

His mouth hangs open. A chunk of bread falls out of the corner and lands on his swollen hand.

She climbs on top of him and starts to feel his chest. "Do you still want me?"

"Uh . . . yeah. Of course."

"Do you want to keep me?"

"What . . ."

Ruth reaches between his legs and grabs his crotch. He gasps. She moves her face closer to his, as if to kiss him, but then positions her mouth by his ear.

"Then keep your fucking job."

She climbs off and goes to the bedroom, closing the door behind her.

Max looks around helplessly, unable to speak or move. He studies the empty hallway, half-expecting her to appear. He gets to his feet and takes a few steps towards the hallway. He looks at the stack of resumes on the table by the door and the envelopes beside them.

"Ruth?" He starts to walk down the hall. "Honey?"

He stops at the bedroom door, raises a hand, and knocks softly.

"Honey? . . . I'm . . . I'm gonna go to the post office to drop off your resumes." He waits for a response. "Okay?"

He puts his ear to the door. "Ruthie? Does that sound okay?"

He tries the handle: locked. "Honey?"

He closes his eyes and rests his forehead on the door. "I love you."

Max Jr. & Max Sr.

Max Jr. unlocks the front door and enters the apartment. He looks around, then slams the door behind him.

"Junior?"

"Yeah."

His father enters the living room.

"Where's Mom?"

"Uh, Mom's not . . . She's sleeping."

"Is she sick?"

"No. Just tired."

Junior studies his father, who avoids his gaze.

"You forgot to do the dishes."

"I didn't forget." He throws his coat on the couch.

"How'd things go with Mel?"

Junior shakes his head in frustration.

"That bad, huh?"

Junior lets himself fall back onto the couch.

"You think you'll see her again?"

"I'd like to."

"You think she'll see *you* again?"

"I don't know. I doubt it."

His father scratches the back of his head and looks around awkwardly. He goes to the kitchen to pour another drink. "Well, try not to worry. Every couple has growing pains. Your mom and I were also pretty . . . *adversarial* when we first met."

"And now look at you."

"What did you do to her?"

"Who?"

"Mel."

"Nothing."

"What did you say to her?"

"I didn't say anything."

"Well, you either said something or you did something. Women don't get pissed over nothing." He raises the glass to Junior and takes a sip. "Correction: women don't get pissed for no reason. They frequently get pissed over nothing."

"Men, on the other hand . . ."

"Are rational."

"Completely and utterly rational."

He ignores his son's sarcasm and takes another sip. "So what did you say to her? Something rational?"

"I didn't . . ."

His father feigns shock. "Something irrational?"

"I asked her . . ."

"To . . . ?"

"You're gonna laugh."

"Probably."

"I asked her to . . . tickle my ear."

A loud, judgmental laugh bursts out of Max. "What?!"

"It's not that weird."

"Yeah, it is."

"The ear is a well-known erogenous zone."

"How did you say it?"

Junior furrows his brow.

"I mean, did you ask politely? Did you say please?"

"I didn't . . . I didn't technically ask . . ."

"You *told* her to tickle your ear? You *ordered*?"

"I wouldn't say ordered."

"What would you say then?"

"I'd say—"

"Tickle my ear." He laughs again. "That's what you'd say."

Junior looks away, embarrassed.

"Don't worry about it. She'll be fine in the morning. Women are—"

"Women aren't anything, Dad. That's your problem. 'Women are x.' 'Women are y.'"

"Women are women, in my experience. Men are men."

"Women aren't anything."

"Don't let your girlfriend hear that."

"And neither are men, for that matter."

"Well, maybe some men."

Junior glares at his father, then looks away. "People are people."

"People are never just people."

"In your experience."

"What other experience is there?"

Junior massages his forehead.

"Look," his father continues, "here's what you do. Buy her some—"

"I don't want your advice."

"I'm just—"

"Or need it. I don't want it. I don't need it. Whatever you suggest, I'll do the opposite."

"Have it your way." He goes back to the kitchen.

"Thank you."

"Just let her sleep on it." He pours another drink. "She'll be fine in the morning."

Junior notices the dishes on the coffee table, covered with crusts and a half-eaten salad. "What happened to Mom?"

"I told you. She's taking a nap."

"She never takes naps."

"Well, she's taking a nap now."

"What did you do to her?"

His father scoffs. "What did I do to her . . ."

Junior gets up, afraid, and walks to the bedroom. He knocks. "Mom? It's Max." When he hears the knob unlock, he opens the door. "Mom?" He goes inside.

His father watches nervously from the living room.

Eventually, Junior returns. "She's not sleeping."

"What's she doing?"

"I think you know what she's doing. The question is why is she doing it."

"What the hell is she doing?" He pushes Junior aside and marches to the bedroom. "Ruth?" He sticks his head in the doorway. "Ruthie?"

Junior watches his father enter and close the door. He glances at the dishes on the table, then at the dishes in the sink. He picks up his father's whiskey glass and examines it, watching the last amber drop roll around the bottom.

He looks down the hall, then picks up his backpack and leaves.

His father returns to the living room. "Junior?" He looks around. When he notices that Junior's backpack is gone, he sits on the couch and turns on the TV.

The sun has begun to set, but the campfire is burning strong. The two Maxs are sitting side by side on a log, roasting marshmallows.

So whaddya think, Maxy? Just us boys, roughin it in the bush. Not a girl in sight.

Who needs em!

Max laughs along with his younger self, the same prideful laugh.

That's ma boy.

Max mutes the TV but keeps watching. He chuckles and shakes his head. "Tickle my ear . . ."

Infamous Endings

John Keats: 26, tuberculosis
Ernest Hemingway: 61, suicide
Sylvia Plath: 30, suicide
Franz Kafka: 40, tuberculosis
Truman Capote: 59, liver disease
Jack Kerouac: 47, liver disease
Dylan Thomas: 39, liver disease
David Foster Wallace: 46, suicide
Virginia Woolf: 59, suicide
Hart Crane: 32, suicide
Bruno Schulz: 50, killed by Nazis
Stephen Crane: 28, tuberculosis
Sarah Kane: 28, suicide
Mark Twain: 74, heart attack
Robert Lowell: 60, heart attack
Georg Trakl: 27, suicide
Lucan: 25, suicide
Yasunari Kawabata: 72, suicide
Arthur Koestler: 77, suicide
Christopher Marlowe: 29, stabbed in the eye
Anton Chekhov: 44, tuberculosis
Emily Bronte: 30, tuberculosis
Honore de Balzac: 51, tuberculosis
D.H. Lawrence: 45, tuberculosis
Katherine Mansfield: 35, tuberculosis
Albert Camus: 46, car crash

Nobodies

A bare stage with a table in the middle, a chair on either side.
Todd, an average-looking undergraduate wearing ripped jeans and a leather jacket, enters from stage right with a script in his hand.

Todd: "Who's there?"

Tucker, another average-looking undergraduate, dressed from head-to-toe in form-fitting plaid, enters from stage left, frustrated.

Tucker: Start again. This time, with passion. You have to stomp in and say it from your gut. Enunciate. Project. Emote.

Todd: We're just writing. We don't have to perform the damn thing.

Tucker: Just trust me. Do it again. You'll see the difference.

Todd rolls his eyes and drags his feet off-stage, letting his sneakers slide and squeak.

Tucker rubs his well-plucked brow as he disappears into the wing. His loafers click like hooves across the floor.

Todd: Ready?
Tucker: Ready!

Todd enters, stomping.

Todd: "WHO'S THERE?"

Tucker walks out casually, adjusting his thick-rimmed glasses.

Tucker: You know, if you're not going to take this seriously . . .

Todd: "Who's there?"
Tucker: With passion.
Todd: Fuck you.

Tucker: There! Say it like that.
Todd: What's so important about "Who's there?"
Tucker: It happens to be the first line from *Hamlet* . . .

Tucker turns to the empty seats and raises an arm, as if on the verge of a soliloquy.

Tucker: . . . when the brave Barnardo stands guard on that fateful night—
Todd: Never mind. Let's just get on with it.
Tucker: Am I keeping you from something?
Todd: Yes. It's Friday night, and instead of getting drunk I'm stuck in an empty, depressing theatre, working on a shitty play with you.
Tucker: *(crossing his arms)* Well, that's not very nice—
Todd: "WHO'S THERE?"
Tucker: Fine.

Tucker closes his eyes and takes a deep breath.

Tucker: "It is I, Godot. I hear you've been waiting for me."

Todd looks at the script, confused.

Todd: "Oh, it's you. At last."
Tucker: A little passion, please . . .

Todd glares at Tucker, then starts flipping through the pages in a panic.

Tucker: "Yes, I'm sorry I was late—"
Todd: *(scanning)* Romeo . . . Antigone . . . Henry the Fourth . . .
Tucker: And that's Pirandello's Henry the Fourth, not Shakespeare's.
Todd: Who's "Shelley"?
Tucker: "The Machine" Levene. *Glengarry Glen Ross.*
Todd: We're supposed to write a normal, realistic play—
Tucker: It *is* realistic.
Todd: How? How is this realistic? To start Act Two, you've got Oedipus making out with Hedda Gabler . . .

Tucker nods enthusiastically.

Todd:	And Act Three finishes with what looks a lot like Macbeth's "Tomorrow and Tomorrow" speech, which is, quote: "sung by Rosencrantz and Guildenstern as they are being hanged by Richard the Third."
Tucker:	Just give it a chance, Todd.
Todd:	And this. "Pause. Hold the pause for twelve and a half seconds."
Tucker:	I thought thirteen was too long.
Todd:	Twelve and a half?
Tucker:	Todd, my young friend—
Todd:	I'm six months older than you.
Tucker:	Todd, my old friend . . .
	He sighs.
Tucker:	. . . read between the lines.
Todd:	I did. You've even written extra lines—in pencil—between the actual lines.
Tucker:	Genius, isn't it?
Todd:	I can't tell. They're written in French.
Tucker:	Exactly.
Todd:	Exactly, what?
Tucker:	That's for you and the audience to decide.
	Todd throws the script at Tucker, who struggles to catch it.
Todd:	The audience doesn't have a script in front of them when they're watching the damn play.
Tucker:	They have to do their homework then.
	Todd sighs and shakes his head. He sits in one of the chairs by the table, leans forward, and massages his temples.
Todd:	You know, I thought working with you on this would make my life easier—
Tucker:	This is good stuff, man.
Todd:	It's bullshit.
Tucker:	It is anything *but* bullshit. It asks timeless questions: "Who am I?" . . . "Who are you?" . . . "Who are we?"

Todd:	"Who gives a shit?"
Tucker:	A fascinating question in itself. What is shit? Why do we give it? To whom do we give it? And why would they want it in the first place?
Todd:	We're starting over.
Tucker:	Come on, man—
Todd:	You said if I came up with the story, you'd write the dialogue. I gave you a simple, realistic story—like the assignment said—and you turned it into something a schizophrenic T.S. Eliot would write.
Tucker:	I decided to go in a different direction.
Todd:	What was wrong with *my* direction?
Tucker:	It was a bit . . . dumb. No offence.
	Todd scoffs.
Todd:	And this is what? Brilliant?
Tucker:	It's original.
	Todd opens his mouth to speak but resists the urge and clears his throat.
Todd:	Look: I just want a decent mark. I know you want to be the next Tom Stoppard or whatever, but I just want to graduate by the time I'm forty.
Tucker:	Yes, I keep forgetting: you're a business major now. Who cares about art if it can't buy you a Porsche?
Todd:	Who cares about art if it can't buy you a meal? Integrity is nice, but it isn't very filling.
	Tucker looks down at the script and curls it into a tube.
Tucker:	I want to keep the scene when King Lear wrestles Uncle Vanya.
Todd:	We're starting over, man. Page one rewrite.
Tucker:	I worked pretty hard on this, you know.
Todd:	I'm sorry to hear that.
Tucker:	Yeah. I'm sure you are.
	Tucker joins Todd at the table. He takes a pen out of his pocket and starts reading through the script, making notes and corrections as he goes.

Todd leans back in his chair and looks up at the unlit lights, the ropes, the catwalk. He follows the pipes along the ceiling, down the wall, and into the darkness of the wing, where he spots a costume rack, filled mostly with broken hangers, and a bin overflowing with props. In the red glow of the exit sign, he can discern the outline of Yorick's skull and Macbeth's severed head, peeking over the top of the bin.

Todd: Did Mulligan ever get back to you on the other play?
Tucker: Not yet.
Todd: When did you give it to him?
Tucker: About a week ago.
Todd: What's taking so long?
Tucker: He's a busy guy. Probably hasn't got to it yet.
Todd: Or he read five pages and put it down.
Tucker: I'm sure he's just busy.
Todd: How long did it take you to read Paula's play?
Tucker: That's different.
Todd: How?
Tucker: Hers was awful.
Todd: What about Carly? You read hers.
Tucker: She's my girlfriend.
Todd groans.
Todd: I know. You need to do something about that.
Tucker: Why? You want her?
Todd: I don't want your leftovers.
Tucker: Good, cause she ain't for sale.
Todd: How is she, by the way?
Tucker: What do you care?
Todd: I'm just curious.
Tucker: She's dead. I shot her and buried her under the stage. Don't tell anyone.
Todd furrows his brow.
Todd: You are not a nice person.
Tucker: I dare ask how Brittney's doing.
Todd: How do you *think* she's doing?

Tucker:	Still haven't called her?
Todd:	You told me not to.
Tucker:	I know. I'm just checking.
Todd:	Thank you for checking.
Tucker:	You're very welcome.
Todd:	I'm touched by your concern.
Tucker:	I touch you as often as I can.
Todd:	So does your girlfriend.
Tucker:	At least I *have* a girlfriend.
Todd:	Girlfriends are overrated.
Tucker:	They're better than boyfriends.
Todd:	How would you know? You've never had one.
Tucker:	I *am* one.

Todd scratches his head, perplexed.

Todd:	I'd go out with you.
Tucker:	I wouldn't.

Tucker turns the page and keeps reading.
Todd picks his fingernails.

Todd:	Guess who I'm going out with tomorrow night.
Tucker:	Your sister?
Todd:	Julie Garner.
Tucker:	Julie Garner?

Todd nods, grinning.

Tucker:	I saw her last night at the bar.
Todd:	Oh yeah?
Tucker:	She was dancing with this guy . . .

Todd's grin fades.

Todd:	Which guy?
Tucker:	Uh, I don't know. Just a random guy.
Todd:	They were dancing?
Tucker:	I'm sure it was nothing.
Todd:	Were they . . . making out or . . .
Tucker:	I don't know. I didn't *see* them make out.

Tucker stops reading and looks up at Todd, who seems lost in his own series of thoughts and confusions.

Tucker:	Mulligan always tells us to write what we know.

He scans the room for guidance.

Tucker:	What do we know?
Todd:	In a metaphysical sense?
Tucker:	In any sense.
Todd:	Video games ... weed ...

Tucker makes a list on the back of the script.

Tucker:	Binge drinking ...
Todd:	Porn ...

Tucker stops writing and examines the list.

Tucker:	I wonder if we could use any of that.
Todd:	Tucker.
Tucker:	Yeah?
Todd:	Did you see Julie with anyone else last night?
Tucker:	No. I told you ...

Todd takes his phone out of his pocket and starts typing.

Tucker:	Are you texting her?

Todd nods.

Tucker:	You think she's ...
Todd:	I don't think anything. I'm just making sure we're still on for tomorrow.
Tucker:	I'm sure everything's fine, man.

Todd finishes the message and puts his phone back in his pocket. He forces a smile.

Todd:	I'm sure too.

Tucker turns the page and keeps reading.

Tucker:	Were you ever going to ask me what *I'm* doing tomorrow night?
Todd:	Nope.
Tucker:	Would you like to know?
Todd:	Not really.
Tucker:	I'm seeing *Othello*.
Todd:	With Carly?
Tucker:	No. Just myself.
Todd:	That's depressing.
Tucker:	Naw, man. Girls are distracting. I'm there to work.
Todd:	Work?
Tucker:	Work. Learn. Absorb. Become inspired.

Todd rolls his eyes.

Tucker: We see each other enough as it is. I don't think she'll mind.
Todd: Your fellow theatre-goers will thank you.
Tucker: What does that mean?
Todd: You know what it means.
Tucker: At least we didn't make out at the dinner table.
Todd: We were drunk!
Tucker: So was everyone else.
Todd: We were in love!
Tucker: So was everyone else.
Todd: What about you and Carly?

Tucker tosses the script on the table.

Tucker: What *about* me and Carly?
Todd: You don't even like each other.
Tucker: I can't believe how jealous you are.
Todd: Of you and Carly?
Tucker: Of me and Carly.
Todd: Two minutes ago, you said she was dead.
Tucker: Sometimes I wish she was. It's natural when you're in love.
Todd: You're insane.
Tucker: Insane with a girlfriend.
Todd: I'll take celibacy over Carly any day.
Tucker: I'm sure the feeling's mutual.
Todd: Can we work on the play, please?
Tucker: I'm sorry. Am I distracting you from your work?
Todd: No. I don't know where I'd be without you.
Tucker: I don't know where you'd be either.
Todd: With Brittney most likely.

Tucker scoffs.

Tucker: Exactly.

He picks up the script and starts reading. After a moment, he puts it down.

Tucker: And speaking of distractions, guess what I saw today.

Todd shrugs.

Tucker:	A nip slip.
Todd:	A nip slip?
Tucker:	A nip slip.
Todd:	Whose nip . . . slipped?
Tucker:	Lauren's.
Todd:	Lauren Pressley?
Tucker:	Lauren. Emmanuel. Pressley.
Todd:	Her middle name's Emmanuel?

Tucker shrugs.

Todd:	You saw Lauren Pressley's tits.
Tucker:	Well, a nipple at least. You know when they lean forward and sometimes their bra sort of falls forward too . . .
Todd:	How old are you again?
Tucker:	You're just jealous.
Todd:	It's 11:30! I want to get this stupid play done, and you're talking about nipples!
Tucker:	Fine. Jesus.

Todd looks away, arms folded.

Todd:	Probably didn't see anything, anyway.
Tucker:	What?
Todd:	I said you probably didn't see anything.
Tucker:	I saw enough.
Todd:	Sure you did.

Tucker stops reading.

Tucker:	Hang on. This should be the play.
Todd:	What should be the play?
Tucker:	This. You know, just talking. No plot, no premise—
Todd:	What would we talk about?
Tucker:	You know, school, girls—
Todd:	Nipples.
Tucker:	Sure, why not? How many plays have you seen with a conversation about nipples?
Todd:	None.
Tucker:	Right. Exactly.

Todd:	There's a reason.
Tucker:	No one writes about nipples. Why? We spend half our day thinking about them.
	Todd furrows his brow.
Todd:	Really?
Tucker:	You know what I mean.
Todd:	So you're suggesting we write a play about nipples.
Tucker:	Come on, man. We could start a revolution here.
Todd:	No one has ever started a revolution writing about nipples.
Tucker:	You clearly haven't read any D.H. Lawrence.
	Todd sighs and leans back in his chair. He takes out his phone and dials a number.
Tucker:	Who are you calling?
Todd:	Julie.
Tucker:	Didn't you just text her?
	Todd ignores him.
Todd:	Voice mail.
	He waits for the tone.
Todd:	Hey Julie, it's me. Just wanted to make sure we're still on for Saturday. Give me a shout when you get a chance.
	Todd puts the phone back in his pocket.
Todd:	Sorry. What were you saying?
Tucker:	I believe we were discussing the merits of—
	Todd's phone vibrates.
Todd:	Hold that thought.
	He checks his new message and sighs.
Tucker:	Is it from Julie?
Todd:	No . . .
	As he reads the message, he starts laughing.
Todd:	Oh, Jesus . . . Why did I give this girl my number . . .
Tucker:	Who is it?
Todd:	A chick from class. Listen to this . . . "Hey, Todd!!! How's it goin? lol Just checkin in to say

	hi. Hope everything's goin well. haha. R u still comin to the club tonite? U said u might come and ur not here and now I'm MAADDD at you. Jk, I'm not mad. But I'm just like wonderin what ur up to. haha. hopefully I'll see u soon. haha lol smiley face".
Tucker:	Does she have some sort of laughing disorder?
Todd:	What do you say to something like that?
Tucker:	Just say you can't come. You've got to work.
Todd:	She won't buy it. She'll find us and drag me out anyway.
Tucker:	Say you've got food poisoning.
	Todd puts his phone on the table.
Todd:	Maybe I just shouldn't say anything.
Tucker:	Don't ignore her. That's such a bitch move.
Todd:	*(picking up the phone)* Yeah. I'll just say I have Chlamydia.
Tucker:	This should be the play.
Todd:	Chlamydia?
Tucker:	No, listen. Let's write what we know. We know what it's like to be two students, dealing with girls, and rejection, and—
Todd:	Nipples?
Tucker:	Sure!
Todd:	Who the fuck's gonna watch that?
	Tucker scoffs.
Tucker:	Don't worry. People will sit through anything these days . . .
Todd:	I'm not sure about *anything* . . .
Tucker:	Todd, it doesn't matter if anyone enjoys it, as long as it's good.
Todd:	But if no one enjoys it, then no one will think it's good.
Tucker:	*We* think it's good.
Todd:	Who the hell are we?
Tucker:	We're writers.
	Todd leans forward and looks suggestively at the script.

Todd:	Not yet.
Tucker:	Then why don't we write about this? About writing a play?
Todd:	Huh?
Tucker:	We write a play about two students trying to write a play for a drama class.
Todd:	Oh, it would be one of those 'plays about a play within a play' sort of things.
Tucker:	Exactly.
Todd:	Those fuckin suck.
Tucker:	No, they don't.
Todd:	What's the point of them?
Tucker:	They're ... commentaries.
Todd:	On?
Tucker:	On the nature of reality. On epistemological limitations. On solipsistic subjectivity. Using a variety of devices to examine illusions—theatrical and otherwise—in highly ironic, insightful and original ways to ultimately produce or provide or propose a conclusion about the paradoxes and dialectics of contemporary postmodernity.
Todd:	So what's the point of them?
	Tucker sighs. He stands, takes out his phone, and starts to walk off-stage.
Todd:	Where are you going?
Tucker:	I'm calling Professor Mulligan.
Todd:	What's *he* going to do?
Tucker:	He might have some ideas.
Todd:	*(as Tucker walks out of earshot)* Make sure you ask him about your play! Twenty bucks says he hasn't read it yet.
	Tucker's footsteps fade.
	Todd lets his gaze wander across the stage. He notices the usual skids and scars, the stains, the evidence of swordfights and spilled blood. Some scars are longer than others, some deeper, while each stain—whether

matte or glossy, spotted or streaked—contains a darkened shade of red.

Todd stands and starts walking. Every few feet he spots tape residue, stripped varnish, chips in the pitch-black paint. He drifts upstage and leans against the wall, surveying his surroundings: the ever-rising curtain, the countless rows of seats, the trapdoor half-hidden beneath the table.

Todd checks his phone: No New Messages.

Frustrated, he starts pacing. He looks at his watch, stands still for a moment, then makes a call.

The phone rings and rings.

No answer. Voice mail.

Todd: Hey, it's me again—it's Todd ... Uh, just wanted to check in ... I know I already called. I just, uh ... just call call me when you get this, okay? All right. Bye.

Todd hangs up. He shakes his head and closes his eyes, trying to stay calm. He places his phone on the table and steps away. He looks off-stage.

Todd: Tucker?

Silence.

Todd: Tucker.

He walks off-stage.

Todd: Tucker!

Todd enters, starts pacing again, then stops and looks at the phone on the table. Reluctantly, he walks over and dials a number. He hesitates before pressing CALL.

No answer. Voice mail.

Todd: Hey. It's almost midnight, and you haven't called me back ... Are we going out tomorrow or ...

Todd covers the phone and hangs his head.

Todd: Look, I just ... I'm not trying to make a big deal out of this. I'd just like to hear from you ... Okay? ... I'll ... I'll talk to you soon ... Bye.

Todd hangs up. He looks off-stage.

Todd: Tucker!

	Silence.
Todd:	*(walking off-stage)* Get out here! Let's finish this fucking play!
	He enters again and tosses the phone on the table. He walks to the other side of the stage, leans against the wall and crosses his arms, glaring at the phone.
Todd:	Tucker!
	He waits for a response, then walks over forcefully and makes another call. He starts pacing.
	No answer. Voice mail.
Todd:	Are you ... Are you ignoring me? I know you have your phone on. I know you got my ...
	He stops pacing and takes a breath.
Todd:	You know what? Don't bother responding.
	He hangs up and looks around indecisively, closing his fist around the phone. He turns to the audience for help, only to find an ocean of empty seats. He lets himself fall back into his chair, lazily, sluggishly, as though he has given up on the proper way to sit. He places the phone on the table and leans back, head hung, staring at his mistake.
Todd:	Fuck.
	Tucker enters with his phone in his hands.
Tucker:	What's your problem? Professor Mulligan thought someone was being murdered.
Todd:	What did he say?
Tucker:	He said if I ever called him at midnight again, he would shove *The Collected Works of Shakespeare* up my—
Todd:	About the play.
Tucker:	He couldn't give us any 'specific ideas.'
Todd:	No, I mean, what did he say about *your* play?
Tucker:	Oh. He hasn't gotten to it yet.
Todd:	What a surprise.
Tucker:	He said he's been really busy, but he's going to try to get to it this weekend.
Todd:	You're being ignored, my friend.

Tucker:	No, I'm not. He's already read part of it—
Todd:	Then you're being rejected.
Tucker:	He's probably only read ten pages—
Todd:	And after five he was probably suicidal. You're lucky he even made it to ten.
Tucker:	Can we just focus on this play? The other one's my business.
Todd:	Well, if the other play's anything like this one . . . What did Mulligan say about *our* play?
Tucker:	Write what you know.

Todd scoffs.

Todd:	Why don't we write about a young aspiring playwright who can't get his own professor to read his play?
Tucker:	He's going to read it.
Todd:	He's just busy.
Tucker:	Why don't we write about *you*? What can we use from *your* perfect life?

Todd's grin disappears.

Tucker:	Brittney? How she broke your little heart. How she can't fucking stand you.
Todd:	Careful, Tucker . . .
Tucker:	How *I* can't fucking stand you.

Tucker starts writing on the back of the script.

Todd:	How about that girl who texted you earlier? The laughing girl.
Tucker:	What about her?
Todd:	Let's write about her. What it's like to be a loser.
Tucker:	She's not a loser.
Todd:	Okay, she's an angel. Can we write about her now?
Tucker:	She's not a loser.
Todd:	Yeah, I got that.

Tucker stops scribbling and scratches out what he wrote.

Tucker:	Never mind.
Todd:	What's wrong with it?

Tucker:	It's too depressing.
Todd:	*Life* is depressing.
Tucker:	That's not a bad title.

Tucker starts writing.

Tucker:	Life . . . Is . . . Depressing . . .
Todd:	I'm serious. Look at us. It's Friday night. We're almost twenty, and look what we're doing.

Tucker points to the script.

Tucker:	I'm working to change that.
Todd:	You think this play will make a difference? You think a grade in a fucking drama class will change anything? It takes more than a university degree—a little piece of paper—to make you rich and famous, Tucker.
Tucker:	I don't want to be rich and famous.
Todd:	Do you know what the success rate is for playwrights?
Tucker:	That depends on your definition of success—
Todd:	It's very low.
Tucker:	Maybe we'll be the lucky ones.
Todd:	Do we look like the lucky ones? We're nobodies. We're not models. We're not trust-fund babies. We're not geniuses. We're average.

Tucker winces at the word 'average.'

Todd:	We'll work hard. We'll do all the right things. We'll keep looking for that lucky break that will always be just around the corner. And it won't make the slightest difference. Because some people aren't meant for success.

Tucker responds with a long silence, almost as long as the speech that inspired it.

Tucker:	That's not a bad speech.

He starts scribbling on the back of the script.

Todd:	What are you doing?
Tucker:	That's a good speech, man. Do you remember any of it?
Todd:	I don't believe this.

Tucker:	*(writing)* Okay, you started with . . .Shit! What did you say? Something about . . . 'Life is depressing.' Great opening line . . . And then . . . Ah, what did you say after that? 'Life is depressing' . . . blah blah blah . . . something about a piece of paper . . . Dammit!
Todd:	What is wrong with you? Didn't you hear anything I just said?
Tucker:	No! *(pointing to the page)* That's clearly the problem!
	He drops the pen and runs his fingers through his hair.
Tucker:	Great . . . That's great. One of the best speeches I've ever heard. Can't remember a word of it.
Todd:	It probably wasn't that good then.
	Tucker rubs his eyes and sighs. He examines the script.
Tucker:	This is impossible . . .
	He leans back in his chair, head slightly hung, legs sprawled out beneath the table.
Tucker:	How about . . .How about this? A play about not having a play. Writing about having nothing to say.
Todd:	Sounds great. Start writing.
	Tucker leans forward, picks up the pen, examines the back of the script, then drops the pen and leans back again.
	They remain frozen in their recumbent positions, staring intensely at nothing in particular.
	Todd's phone starts to vibrate on the table. He makes no effort to answer it.
Tucker:	You gonna get that?
	Todd doesn't respond.
Tucker:	It might be Julie.
	Todd remains still. Tucker reaches out and slides the phone across the table.
Tucker:	Don't ignore people.
	Todd leans forward slowly, checks the number, then leans back.

Todd:	It's the girl from class.
Tucker:	The laughing girl?
	Todd nods. The phone keeps vibrating.
Tucker:	I think she wants to talk to you.
	Todd doesn't move. Tucker starts flipping through the script.
Tucker:	Is it really that bad?
Todd:	Sorry, man.
	Tucker reads a section and crosses it out. He turns the page. After scanning a few lines, he draws an X through the entire page.
Todd:	Start writing.
Tucker:	Huh?
Todd:	"Act One. A bare stage with a table in the middle, a chair on either side."
	Tucker starts writing, confused.
Todd:	"Todd, an average-looking undergraduate wearing ripped jeans and a leather jacket, enters from stage right with a script in his hand. Todd: 'Who's there?' Tucker, another average-looking undergraduate, dressed from head-to-toe in form-fitting plaid, enters from stage left, frustrated."
	Tucker looks up at Todd and grins.
Tucker:	"Tucker: 'Start again. This time, with passion.'"
	Smiling, Todd nods towards the script. Tucker starts writing.

(More) Infamous Endings

George Orwell: 47, tuberculosis
Paul Celan: 49, suicide
Novalis: 29, tuberculosis
Margaret Laurence: 60, suicide
Primo Levi: 58, suicide
William Faulkner: 67, heart attack
F. Scott Fitzgerald: 44, heart attack
Friedrich Schiller: 46, tuberculosis
Laurence Sterne: 55, tuberculosis
Weldon Kees: 41, suicide
Tennessee Williams: 71, choked on a bottle cap
Anne Sexton: 45, suicide
John Berryman: 57, suicide
Vladimir Mayakovsky: 36, suicide
Frederico Garcia Lorca: 38, killed by fascists
Henry David Thoreau: 45, tuberculosis
Yukio Mishima: 45, suicide
John Kennedy Toole: 31, suicide
Charlotte Mew: 59, suicide
Moliere: 51, tuberculosis
Thomas Wolfe: 38, tuberculosis
Anne Bronte: 29, tuberculosis
Elizabeth Barrett Browning, 55, tuberculosis
Petronius: 39, suicide
Walter Benjamin: 48, suicide
Nathaniel West: 37, car crash

Cormac McCarthy Orders a Pizza

Operator:	Thank you for calling Papa Jerry's. What can I get for you today?
McCarthy:	A pie of average size with bloodred medallions atop a lavalike layer of bubblings that reaches in vain for the stony burnt crust.
Operator:	Beg your pardon?
McCarthy:	A medium pepperoni.
Operator:	Will this be delivery or pick up?
McCarthy:	Depends on the position of the godless sun by which men have come to tell time and therefore by which time has come to tell men of that which has come to pass and may yet come to pass since time is a smokedarkened nexus of chimes and ticks that only reveals its full allotment after the fall of the final stroke.
Operator:	Uh . . .
McCarthy:	What time is it?
Operator:	10:32.
McCarthy:	Delivery, then. I dare not venture forth into the nameless night from which nothing save wolves emerge as emissaries of a void beyond reckoning.
Operator:	Can I get your address?
McCarthy:	I live at the intersection of nihilistic despair and aesthetic idealism.
Operator:	Is that a house or an apartment?
McCarthy:	House. 343 Holden Drive.
Operator:	Can I get a name for the order?
McCarthy:	Cormac.
Operator:	Kermit?
McCarthy:	Cormac.
Operator:	Like the frog?
McCarthy:	*(sighs)* Sure. Like the frog.

Operator:	Would you like to try our Spicy Garlic Fun Sticks for 3.99?
McCarthy:	Negative. Eternally negative.
Operator:	And how would you like to pay?
McCarthy:	With my soul and with the souls of all who face the icy blackness of the world in its final turning with the stubbornstoic hope of a deafmute monk who hears God's silence and responds in kind.
Operator:	We take cash and credit.
McCarthy:	Credit.
Operator:	Okay, Kermit. The time is now 10:34. Your order is guaranteed in 30 minutes or it will be free. Thank you for calling Papa Jerry's.
McCarthy:	Thank you for *being* Papa Jerry's. I salute your courage.

The Incomprehensible Here

I spot Father O'Neill in the wine section, flirting with a full-bodied Pinot. No cart. No basket. No foresight. The O'Neill I know isn't a one-bottle shopper.

Nor is he a snazzy dresser. Yet here he is in a suit. A sleek, tailored, ungodly black suit. The kind that Satan would wear. Or Dorian Gray. The stitching never weakens; the fabric never fades. Even the folds and creases are lined with grace.

O'Neill mumbles something to the Pinot. Something with consonants, but no vowels. As if he were speaking in tongues.

I duck into the aisle, close enough to hear, yet far enough to keep out of sight. The shelf conceals everything below my chin; the Chardonnay selection obscures the rest. If he moves right along the back wall instead of left, I'll be exposed, but still out of reach. If he wants to hurt me, he'll have to throw a bottle.

But maybe hiding is absurd. He wouldn't recognize me with the beard, let alone the shoulder-length hair. I hardly recognize him without his costume. Or, for that matter, his comb-over. Ten years ago his hair was wispy and weak; now it's slicked back in silver lines across his skull.

O'Neill picks up a new bottle, hums a tune and sways, as if slow dancing. Is he drunk already? It's not even 5:30. Perhaps he's just giddy. Maybe he saved a confessor from suicide and is still basking in his post-priestly glow. Maybe he's heading to a late-night prayer meeting, or a date with Sister Roberta.

He mutters sweet nothings as he feels up the label. Then his fingers stop. Something must be wrong with the vintage.

"Not quite my type," he mumbles, dumping the bottle in the rack. He picks up another. "Yessss," he says. "You're the one I've been looking for."

★ ★ ★

I only spoke to O'Neill on birthdays, after the Big Man gave unwanted gifts. (For my Sweet Sixteen, He sent heartbreak. For the Big Two-O, the Big C. And for my quarter-life crisis, an end-of-life crisis.) Life, I assumed, had a satisfaction guarantee, an extended warranty on all products, regardless of price, and if I was unhappy, I should visit O'Neill in the Complaints Department. At sixteen, my grievance was minor—damaged packaging, easily fixed—but at twenty, it was major: faulty wiring, defective batteries. Unfixable, but quickly exchanged. At twenty-four, I told the Big Man to go to hell. Missing parts. Irreplaceable. No refund. No exchange. Just grievance.

Sixteen-Year-Old Me, the victim of a recent dumping, was no match for O'Neill. He may have been an intellectual lightweight, but I was only a featherweight. If I ever wanted to beat him at his own game, I would have to bulk up my brain. So I began reading books with big words and long titles, hoping to pack on pounds of knowledge, strengthen my stamina, and master the art of argumentation. Between meals of Plato and Schopenhauer, I snacked on Sudoku, and after two years of training, O'Neill and I were evenly matched. After two more—during which I discovered chess, Vitamin B, and crossword puzzles—I was a full-fledged welterweight, if not a border-line middleweight.

Bout One may have been a one-sided lecture, but Bout Two was a cross-bearing debate. O'Neill began by beating out my latest grievance, even though it was written across my hair-speckled scalp. He told me to speak my mind and say what was in my heart, since the Big Man knew everything anyway. I didn't mention that what was in my heart rarely matched what was in my head, nor did I note the redundancy of his position as a spiritual middleman. I simply asked him why God would condemn a twenty-year-old to death. I had never committed a serious crime, I went to church more often than most Christians, and I frequently treated my friends and family with respect. Even my three ex-girlfriends had nice things to say about me, generally speaking. What did I do to deserve cancer?

Instead of answering, O'Neill lowered himself into the pew and placed a ring-less hand on my shoulder. He reminded me that

God was higher than we were, that He asked for love, not understanding.

"He'd have to be pretty high," I replied, "to ask for one without the other."

O'Neill's hand fell away. He quoted Proverbs 9:10: *The fear of the Lord is the beginning of wisdom.*

"Just as the fear of logic is the beginning of delusion."

He said I should be grateful for what I had, since things could always be worse. For most of the planet, things *were* worse.

"And for that I should be grateful?"

He didn't respond. Probably because he agreed but could never admit it.

Luckily, my cancer was treatable, but it caused a lot of anxiety at the time. It was as if God were teasing me, forcing me to be grateful for an illness that could have always been worse. For months—before, during, and after my treatment—I dedicated myself to hating Him, and He rewarded me with life. After all, death would have been a gift; He knew I wanted to meet Him face-to-face.

My indignation grew as I recovered, and where others saw mercy, I saw mockery. I wouldn't rest until I beat Him at His own game, so I practiced on my parents and turned the kitchen into a court room. They defended the Big Man more adamantly than O'Neill ever would or could, but in their few moments of weakness I managed to convince them to take up the cross against their Lord and Savior.

For every stone I threw at the sky I expected a boulder to fall in return. But months passed, then years, and nothing happened. Eventually, I ended my crusade and turned my mind to more important matters, like girls and school. I not only forgave God, but when things went well I actually thanked Him. Genuinely. Earnestly. And that's when the boulder fell.

By then, it had been five years since my last bout with Father "Middleman" O'Neill. We didn't speak at my parents' funeral, but I left a note on the altar requesting a rematch. He had heard my eulogy; I had heard his sermon. For the moment, there was nothing more to say.

★ ★ ★

O'Neill moves along the back wall, and I move with him, hopping from aisle to aisle, crouching behind promotional displays and racks of discount Rieslings.

Even his walk is different, a sober glide instead of a stumble. His eyebrows are longer too. They peel up and away from his face, either reaching for the heavens or fleeing their earthly constraints. But the real mystery is his suit, which O'Neill couldn't afford even if he stole from the collection plate. Why would he want it anyway? Isn't there some kind of after-hours dress code? Or has he retired from the Complaints Department?

So many questions, doomed to go unanswered. If only I had the nerve to confront him.

When I was younger, I liked to sum up my enemies in a sentence, reducing entire lives to a single subject, verb, and thought. Girls had daddy issues; boys had mommy issues; O'Neill had whiskey issues. (And daddy issues of a more metaphysical kind.) But something about O'Neill eluded my reductions. For every cliché, I found a contradiction—one that would unravel my tidy theory. The way he sighed before speaking. The way he broke the bread and poured the wine, as if dining at his own Last Supper. The length and tone of his silences, hinting at a sermon beyond speech.

I had known O'Neill since I was five or six, when my parents decided to abandon their pagan pastimes and get cosy with God. I never quite shared their faith, but I had a hard time putting the Big Man out of my head. Even if I knew He wasn't there, a part of me always believed He was—especially when I wished He wasn't. In a good mood, I was an atheist; in a bad mood, a believer; in an average mood, an agnostic. Most of the time, my mood was average, which made life hard to navigate.

"A Godless world is an indifferent world," I once told him, "but at least it isn't cruel."

O'Neill replied that the world was cruel, with or without God's help.

His fervor may have waned as his years advanced, but he drank only enough to numb the pain of his disbelief. Whenever

I spoke with him, I could smell the sacrament on his breath, yet it didn't seem to affect his performance. The parables and the platitudes were still intact, chiselled into his mind alongside the doubts and the regrets.

According to some, O'Neill hid flasks around the church: in the vestibule, under the altar, behind the crucifix. The only confirmed location was the last. One Sunday, after catechism, an altar boy saw O'Neill remove a black object from the back of the cross, just inches below the feet and the nail.

"Is that one of those GPS tracking things?" the boy asked, assuming it was meant to protect our Lord and Savior from thieves.

"It's a container," O'Neill said, slipping the flask into his robes.

When asked what the container contained, O'Neill replied without hesitation: "Holy water."

★ ★ ★

O'Neill stops at a tasting booth, presumably to sample each bottle with poise and restraint, to sniff and swirl and sip. However, when the tattooed clerk gestures to the red, O'Neill bites his lip, waves an absolving hand, and keeps walking.

Who is this impostor, and what has he done with O'Neill? Why is he here, if not to stock up on holy water? Maybe he knows that I'm following him. Maybe he's following me. Maybe the Big Man sent him.

Is O'Neill here to drop the next boulder? How does divine intervention usually work? Am I supposed to confront him, or is he supposed to approach me? Does it matter? What will happen if I just avoid him? My parents are already dead, and I renounced everyone else who matters to me. Maybe my cancer is back. But how the hell would *he* know that?

O'Neill turns suddenly, as if he forgot something, and walks toward me. I duck behind the nearest display rack, but before I can peek over the top, I hear a familiar voice:

"Charlie? Is that you?"

★ ★ ★

Compared to Bouts One and Two, Bout Three went well. Perhaps too well.

The day of reckoning summoned clear, windless skies and springtime temperatures. Ideal for a round of golf or a picnic, but not for an epic rematch. I wanted hurricane winds, sheets of rain, lightning swatting planes out of the sky. Something to match the gravitas of the occasion. Something to echo the rage constricting my heart, heating my veins. I felt like a warrior on the march to a coliseum, eager to embrace another victory or accept a final defeat.

I assumed that O'Neill was still a lightweight, but perhaps he had changed. Maybe he rediscovered his passion for God and now put on his collar with pride. Maybe he hummed his hymns with gusto and recited his sermons with delight. Maybe the blood of Christ was now reserved for worshippers only—or, at the very least, consumed in moderation. *Blessed are the sober, for they shall inherit the car keys.* I saw that on a bumper sticker in the parking lot and prayed that it belonged to O'Neill. But I couldn't imagine a man of the cloth driving a mini-van.

As I entered the church, I vowed to stay calm and engage O'Neill on the most profound levels of theology, but when I saw him sway down the aisle with his sunken, world-weary face, I knew what was about to happen.

"You should be happy," he said, easing into the pew. "Your parents are in Heaven."

"I'd be happier if they were here."

"I know. But rest assured they're with God now."

"Well, can you ask God to give them back? They weren't in any rush to join Him."

"In their hearts, they were."

"And in their minds, they weren't. I wonder which organ is more relevant."

"I know it's hard to understand, but this is all part of God's plan."

"And the drunk driver, who got off with a fine—how does *he* fit into God's plan?"

O'Neill cleared his throat and forced a patronizing smile. "Do you want to live the rest of your life in anger?"

"Gladly. Any other way would be an insult."

"They wouldn't want you to live like this either."

"I don't really see an alternative."

"That's because you've turned away from God, my son. Away from your fellow man—"

"If I ever see 'my fellow man' again, I'll do a lot more than turn away from him. And if I see God, and He's dumb enough to let me anywhere near those Pearly Gates, He better buckle up. Eternity's going to be a bumpy ride with me in the back seat."

I knew how silly I sounded, but I didn't care. I was striking a blow for divine justice, even if the only thing I could hit was air. Dusty, holy, otherworldly air. The air of salvation and hypocrisy. The air of divine justice.

After twenty-five years of life, I had concluded that there was nothing just about divinity and nothing divine about justice. There was only The Incomprehensible Hereafter and The Incomprehensible Here, with little in common besides middle names. The Hereafter was, is, and always will be, the grand enigma: endlessly frustrating, perpetually fascinating, permanently out-of-reach. Like a lover who justifies their contradictions through mystery and blames their partner for their own flights of infidelity. The Here, on the other hand, was more accessible but no less absurd, and it seemed to be occupied by two types of people: The Lucky and The Unlucky—or, according to The Unlucky, The Unlucky and The Super Unlucky. Yet such pessimism was unrealistic, for many people could count themselves among The Lucky: those who had not yet been born, and those who were already dead.

"What about your parents?" O'Neill asked. "What happens if you see them?"

"Somehow I don't think that will be an issue. Your God and my fellow man have made sure of that."

"He's your God too, you know. For better or worse."

"Well, let Him know I want a divorce." I stood and grabbed my jacket. "I met someone with horns and a tail who seems to get me."

"It's up to you to close the wound, my son. No one can do it for you."

I started to walk away.

"I'm not your son. Father."

Was that the best God could do? Or did He think so little of me that He wouldn't even grant me a worthy opponent? Either way, I showed the Big Man what a real man looked like, and I awaited his judgment with furious glee.

A week later, I received an unsigned, wine-stained letter with no return address:

> *You arrogant, delusional brat.*
> *The world does not revolve around you.*
> *Grow up.*

Years passed. I cut off my friends, broke up with my girlfriend, and abandoned my dreams, fearing what might happen if I had something to lose. Death was not going to come from above—I knew that—but it could still arrive from the side, from the front, from behind. And I would never see it coming. God was a dog that did not need to bark; His bite spoke for itself.

But I'm thirty-three, and I'm still waiting to feel it.

★ ★ ★

As O'Neill approaches, his pants rattle. Car keys. Loose change. The Holy Flask.

"I thought it was you," he says, tilting his head. "What are you doing down there?"

"Uh, just tying my shoe."

I stand, meeting him eye to eye. He studies my hippie hair, my beard, my surf shorts. His gaze lingers, however, on my flip-flops.

"How are you?" he asks, sizing up his opponent. "You look . . ."

"Like a homeless Jesus?"

He laughs and nods. "I like your sandals."

"I like your suit."

"Isn't it nice?" He runs his hand over the fabric. "My brother was a tailor."

I ask if the Big Man has a dress code.

"I'm on sabbatical," he replies. "Returning in April."

I point to the bulge in his pocket and ask if he still sticks it behind Jesus.

He furrows his pious brow.

"The flask," I explain. "Do you still . . ."

He reaches into his pocket and pulls out a steel crucifix.

"It's for my niece," he says. "I'm on my way to her birthday party."

I look at the bottle in his other hand. "Does your niece drink Pinot?"

"Her parents do."

"What about her uncle?"

"Eight years sober." He even shows me his AA token, a bronze medallion the size of a poker chip. *TO THINE OWN SELF BE TRUE*, it says, along with *UNITY, SERVICE, RECOVERY* and the roman numeral for eight.

His guard is down, his chin exposed. This is my chance for a knockout punch.

"You should come by the church sometime," he says. "It'd be nice to see a familiar face."

A left hook, out of nowhere! My mind staggers back. I reach for theories to break my fall, some rationale to explain his demeanor. His eyes seem sober, his smile sincere. But "seem" is the key word. I shouldn't be fooled by his cheek-turning. It's just another tactic in his arsenal. He knows I'll win if we fight.

Or maybe he's indifferent. Maybe the Big Man is indifferent too. Maybe they have always been indifferent, and my epic battles were nothing more than daydreams, confined to my head. Does O'Neill even remember our last encounter? And, if so, does he care? Have I wasted the best years of my life on a delusion?

You should come by the church sometime, he says. (What the hell does that mean?) *It'd be nice to see a familiar face.*

I have one last chance to duck and deflect, to salvage my struggle.

I tell O'Neill, "You know, I just might."

He smiles and shakes my hand. "Take care, Charlie."

"See you around, Father."

And then he leaves. No boulder. No Bout Four.

Ping Pong

And I don't want her coming to my funeral./ What?/ She's not invited./ Of course she's invited. She's my mother./ Sorry, but that's non-negotiable./ She has to come./ Why?/ For me./ Whose funeral is it again? Who's the one in the coffin? She's still my mother./ That's terrific./ Not to mention your ex-wife./ Key word: ex./ I want her to be there./ I don't really care what you want. It's not your funeral./ You won't even . . ./ What?/ You won't even be there./ I'll be there. I won't be breathing, but I'll be there./ You know what I mean./ She's not invited. Period. End of discussion. I'm not going to let that bitch—/ Watch it./ That *person* . . . infect my life again./ Technically speaking, it's not your life./ It's my death. It's *my* death. Not yours. Not hers. Mine./ How do you expect me to tell her that? How do you expect me to call my mother and—/ Not my problem./ It *is* your problem. You're the one creating it./ No, I'm the one concluding it./ Why are you being such a—/ Prick? Because that *person* is poison./ I wasn't going to say "prick."/ She's fucking poison, and I'm not gonna let her—/ She won't—/ End of discussion. She's not coming. I'm telling Freddy./ Telling him what?/ Not to let her in. I'll post police if I have to./ I'm pretty sure you can't—/ I can do whatever the fuck I want./ Not when you're dead./ Especially when I'm dead. I'll put it in writing. I'll get a restraining order./ Stop being ridiculous./ I don't want her there. Period./ Why?/ Many reasons./ Give me one./ IT'S MY FUCKING FUNERAL./ I understand that./ You don't. You think it's about you. As usual, you think it's all about you./ Not as usual. And, yes, it *is* about me. It's about everyone./ It's about *me*. I'm the one in the coffin. I'm the one who's dead. And I'll suck the devil's dick before I let her walk through the door./ So you've decided on an indoor service?/ Fuck off./ And I thought you wanted to be cremated. What's all this shit about a coffin?/ You know exactly what I'm saying, smart ass./ I know what you're saying; I don't know why you're saying it./ It doesn't matter./ It matters to me./ Well, you're just gonna have to live with that./ Now, who's the selfish one?/ I have a right to be selfish. It's my fucking—/ Funeral. I get it./ Thank you./ But you're not the only one in attendance. In fact, from a medical perspective, you're not in attendance at all./ I can't believe you're doing this./ Ditto./ I'm fucking dying, and you're . . . After all that's happened./ What's happened? I still don't know what's happened./ You know perfectly well./ I don't./ I'm not getting into it. The point is simple. Ruth. Isn't. Coming. She's been out of my life. She'll be out of my death./ I can't handle this./ *I* CAN'T HANDLE THIS. YOU THINK THIS IS HARD FOR YOU? *I'M* THE ONE WHO'S FUCKING DYING./ I understand that—/ *I'M* THE ONE WHO HAS TO WASTE AWAY, WONDERING HOW SHE'S GOING TO FUCK ME OVER WHEN I'M NOT EVEN ALIVE TO DEFEND MYSELF./ She's not going to—/ I can't believe it. After all these years, she's finally going to kill me. It's what she's always wanted, and she's finally going to do it. And you're going to help her.

We need to talk, and you're not going to like what I have to say./ What do you mean?/ It's about Dad. About his funeral./ His funeral? Did something happen?/ No, no, he's fine./ Thank God./ Well, not fine, but you know . . ./ What happened?/ Nothing *happened*. We had a talk./ About his funeral?/ Yeah./ Does he want me to give a eulogy? Oh God. I don't know if I—/ He doesn't want you to come./ What?/ He doesn't—/ Why?/ He didn't say./ He said something./ He said . . . he has his reasons./ Which are?/ He didn't say./ But why would he—/ I don't think he likes you very much./ He said that? He said he doesn't like me?/ Not in those words./ What did he say?/ He didn't say anything. That's what I'm telling you./ Then why are you saying he doesn't like me?/ Because he doesn't. It's no big secret./ What did he tell you?/ He said you can't come to the funeral./ Well . . ./ His words, not mine./ Well, screw him. He doesn't get to decide who—/ I'm afraid he does./ He can't control me./ That's not what *he* thinks./ Well, he can think whatever he wants. It's too damn bad./ This isn't really up for debate./ You're right. I'm not going to debate a thing. I'm just going to do what I want./ I won't let you./ What?/ I won't let you. Uncle Freddy won't let you./ What's *he* going to do?/ You won't be allowed inside./ He can't control who attends his funeral. Is he crazy?/ Probably. Either way, you're not invited./ It's a funeral. No one's "invited." You just show up./ Well, you're not showing up./ I'll show up wherever I goddamn please./ No, you won't. I won't let you./ Why are you being like this?/ I'm not being like anything. I'm just delivering a message./ You don't want me to come. You just said so./ No, I didn't. I said—/ I know what you said./ Look, I'm sorry. I really am. But I'm not the bad guy here./ You're one of them./ How? I haven't done anything./ You're doing plenty. As usual, you're taking his side./ Stop with the "as usual." I'm tired of—/ It's true. You always take his side. You even sound like him when you talk./ Stop making this about you. This has nothing to do with you. Or me, for that matter. This is what he wants, and it's what he'll get. It's my job to honor his wishes./ "Honor his wishes." Okay, Junior./ Don't call me that./ It's your name, isn't it?/ He says the same thing about you, by the way./ What?/ That I sound like you when I fight with him./ Of course he does. It's because he's—/ Stop. I'm not doing this. I refuse to be your ping pong ball./ Ping pong ball?/ Back and forth, back and forth. Ever since I could speak./ Don't be so melodramatic./ I'm tired of it. I refuse to go back to that. I'm twenty-nine, and I'm not going to be your punching bag./ Punching bag?/ Or his, for that matter./ Punching bag or ping pong ball? I'm confused./ I'm too old for this shit./ Then put him on the phone./ He doesn't want to talk to you. I don't want to talk to you either./ Oh, that's nice./ About this, I mean./ Sure./ I'm just passing on information. Do with it what you will./ "Do with it what you will." And you say you don't sound like him./ Look, it is what it is./ "It is what it is."/ Stop it./ He's so selfish. He thinks the funeral's for him. He's dead. He doesn't matter. It's for his survivors. It's for the people he leaves behind./ Which doesn't include you./ We were married for eighteen years./ And you haven't spoken in ten./ So?/ He doesn't want you there./ I wouldn't be there for him. I'd be there for you./ I'll be fine./ And for me./ You'll be fine too./ And so will he. So will everyone else./ No, they won't./ Well, that's too damn bad. I'm gonna do what I want, and everyone else will have to live with it./ *I'm* going to have to live with it. That's the point. You make your demands, he makes his, and I get stuck in the middle./ Don't blame me for that./ I'm blaming both of you./ Fine. Blame whoever you want. I'm still coming.

Baby, what's wrong?/ Nothing. I just wanted to hear your voice./ Is everything okay?/ Not really./ Is there anything I can do?/ No, just talk to me. Tell me about your day./ Are you still at the hospital?/ Yeah. I'm down in the caf./ Is your dad okay?/ Yeah, he's fine. Tell me about your day./ Uh. Are you sure?/ Yeah, go ahead./ Okay. Well, first I went shopping. Got a new pair of jeans. Had a bagel in the food court. Salmon and cream cheese on pumpernickel—/ I miss you./ What's going on, baby? Is your dad okay?/ Yes and no./ Did you talk about his funeral?/ Yeah./ How did it go?/ Not well./ I'm sorry, Maxy Bear./ It's okay./ Do you want to talk about it?/ Not really. But I do want to hear about your day./ No, you don't. My day was boring./ Boring beats mine./ Yeah./ I wish you were here. I'd give you a big smooch on the lips./ Ooooo./ And a hug./ *And* a hug? Lucky me./ Two hugs, if you play your cards right./ Sweeeeet./ And a bum squeeze./ Ooooo. You're making me wet./ That was easy./ Annnnd now I'm dry./ Woops./ Well done, Mister Sex Pants./ *Captain* Sex Pants./ I thought you liked Mister./ I changed my mind./ Well, then . . ./ Is that okay?/ Aye aye, Captain.

So I talked to mom./ Wonderful./ And she's not too happy./ I can imagine./ She wants to come to your funeral./ That's unfortunate./ Yes, it is. Because I'm the one who has to deal with her./ Yep./ I'm the one who has to pay the price for your bullshit./ Take it up with Ruth. She's the one intruding./ Intruding, to you. No one else cares./ Fred doesn't want her there either./ Only because *you* don't want her there. He's acting on your behalf./ As he should./ Don't make this about the rest of the family. It's about you and her./ It's about *you* and her. She's gonna drag you through this. She's going to whine and bitch and complain until she gets her way, because that's how she operates. Always has, always will. She's going to manipulate and guilt-trip and mindfuck her way into getting what she wants, because she knows you can't fight back./ Says you./ And the worst part is, she doesn't even *want* to come. She doesn't give a shit about me. About saying goodbye. She said goodbye ten years ago, when she . . ./ What?/ The point is, she's selfish. She just wants to get her way. No matter what it is or what it costs. No matter who it hurts. All that matters is that it's hers. Especially if someone tells her it's not./ I think you're being a bit paranoid./ I think you're being a child. Which is exactly why she can use you./ Calm down. No one's using anyone./ I wish that were true./ You know, you sound like a—/ Junior./ I told you not to—/ *Max*. Listen. I know she's your mother, but she's also my wife—/ Ex-wife./ And you simply don't know her like I do./ Just as *you* simply don't know her like *I* do./ True./ "Husband" and "son" are not the same./ Yeah, the husband stands a chance./ I'm glad I didn't inherit your cynicism./ She's been doing this since you were born, and she's doing it again. Only this time I won't be around to protect you./ I think I'll be fine on my own./ I'm not so sure./ You seem to think I'm unaware of what's happening. Of my position in all this. I'm not. I'm very aware. You haven't said a single thing I don't already know. Or haven't considered./ Good. So we're agreed./ We're not agreed. I'm just letting you know. And there's a difference between knowing something and being able to do something about it./ As long as you're aware./ Why? What good is awareness if it doesn't help you? If it only reminds you how helpless you are?/ I'd rather be self-aware and self-loathing than blissfully ignorant and destructive. Just ask your mother./ You're no less ignorant. No less destructive. If you were, you'd let this go./ She's the bad guy, not me./ You're both the bad guy./ According to you./ It's a reasonable request, you know. She wants to attend your funeral. Big deal. Why make everything into a battle?/ Because I can. Because it's what she expects./ Well, how about you subvert expectations by doing the right thing?/ I *am* doing the right thing./ The noble thing. Fuck right and wrong. This is about—/ The path of least resistance. Your favourite path./ I've spent too much time on the other path. You have too./ Then a few more weeks won't kill me./ "A few more weeks" is why you're here. Your inability to let things go./ *She* is why I'm here./ It takes two to tango, Father Dearest. She fucked up; you fucked up. Why don't we bury the hatchet and call it a draw?/ Because it's what she wants. A draw means defeat./ It's what she wants—maybe—but it's not what she's expecting./ I hope it's not what *you're* expecting, because you're going to be disappointed./ Hoping, not expecting. It's never too late to change./ I'm not the one who needs to change, Sonny./ Maybe. Maybe not. But you're the one who can./ So can she. Why aren't you yelling at her?/ I was. I will. But right now I'm yelling at you./ I don't want her infecting my family. Not to mention my friends./ Then don't invite her. But let her come./ I can't stop her from coming. It's a free country, last time I checked.

What the hell is his problem?/ He's meeting you half-way./ What a saint./ It's the best you're going to do./ If he doesn't want me there, I'm not going to go./ Uh. Okay. Great./ Why would I? The only reason I'd go is for him./ Good. I'll let him know./ You sound happy./ I'm relieved./ That I'm not going?/ That there won't be a problem./ There wouldn't be a problem if I went./ That's debateable./ It sounds like you don't want me to go./ I *do* want you to go. I also want to do what he wants./ And avoid a fight./ I don't think that's unreasonable./ Avoiding fights is kind of your thing./ Don't start with me./ I'm serious. You're always taking his side, breaking us up—/ You broke yourselves up./ I mean the fights. Breaking up the fights./ Someone had to do it./ Maxy Junior. Defender of the Wounded Patriarch./ I'm trying to create some peace./ Peace and quiet. That's all you want./ Your point being . . ./ Once again, it's all about you./ No, actually it's all about *you*. Going the one place you're not wanted, not because you want to but because you can. You *think* you can./ I know I can, and he's not going to stop me./ I thought you weren't going./ I changed my mind./ For fuck's sake . . ./ Watch your mouth. I'm still your mother./ Fuck my mouth, and fuck my mother./ Watch it, brat./ I'M NOT YOUR FUCKING BRAT!

And I'm not his either! I'm twenty-nine years old!/ You've got your father's temper. At least that hasn't changed./ What did you do to him?/ What do you mean?/ He keeps talking about this thing that happened, but he won't say what it is./ I divorced him. That's what happened./ He says he divorced you./ Of course he does. He's been saying it since I gave him the papers./ You let him say it./ I didn't want to torture the guy. I just wanted to move on. And I have./ He hasn't./ Clearly./ So where does that leave us?/ In terms of what?/ In terms of the funeral./ I don't know. I'm meeting someone for dinner./ Someone special?/ What do you care?/ I'm just curious./ Are *you* curious, or is Max curious?/ Wait, why would he cover it up? It's no secret you're divorced./ Because he's embarrassed. Because I got away. Because I was his sure thing, and I told him no. I was the one thing he thought he could control. It's about ego, not about me. His puny little manhood./ What would he say if I said that?/ You know what he'd say. He'd say I'm a scheming little . . . *whatever*, who doesn't have a respectable thought in her head./ I doubt he'd say "respectable."/ I was paraphrasing.

I'm sorry, baby. I can't believe they're putting you in the middle of this./ I know. It's ridiculous./ Do you want me to come down?/ No, it's okay./ I wish there was something I could do./ Just keep doing what you're doing./ All right. Whaddya want to talk about?/ I don't know. Anything. How about . . . chemistry? Let's name the elements of the periodic table./ Wanna know what I'm wearing?/ Hydrogen, helium, lithium—/ Nothing. I just stepped out of the shower./ Oxygen. Nice./ I'm still wet./ H2O./ And, woops, I just dropped my towel./ So you *were* wearing something./ A towel doesn't count./ Sure, it does. I was picturing . . ./ What?/ I can't really say. I'm, uh . . . still in the caf./ Go somewhere private./ The bathroom?/ How about the coma ward?/ Very funny./ Sorry./ It's okay./ I can't believe they're doing this to you. It's hard enough . . ./ Yeah./ They're so selfish./ I can't really blame them./ Yes, you can. You should. It's *their* problem. They should be the ones to deal with it./ I know./ Sorry. I know you're just trying to . . . get through this./ You're right though. They think it's all about them. They don't seem to get that selfishness is a double-edged sword./ Hmm?/ When you accuse someone else, you're doing it too. "Stop thinking about yourself, and think about me."/ Which is selfish as well./ They don't seem to understand that. He thinks his funeral's about him; she thinks it's about everyone else./ But mostly her./ Entirely her./ What about you? Why should you accommodate them when they don't accommodate you?/ Good question.

That's not what I said./ Huh?/ I didn't say she could come. I said I can't stop her./ Right. She's not invited, but she can come./ No, she can't come./ You just said you couldn't stop her./ Doesn't mean she can come./ She *can* come. You're saying she shouldn't./ I'm saying what I said. She can do what she wants./ Which means she can come./ Which means I can't stop her./ And neither can anyone else./ That's up to them./ No, it's up to you. I want you to call Uncle Freddy and tell him not to get in her way if she—/ I'm not telling him shit./ Why?/ I don't want to./ That's a mature response./ Since when have I cared about the maturity of my responses?/ Better late than never./ Freddy can do what he wants. So can the others./ I don't want an incident./ Then tell her not to come./ I did. She's not going to listen./ Then that's her problem./ No, it's mine./ Then tell her not to come./ Look, that day is going to be hard enough if all goes well. If everyone's getting along and no one drops the coffin. It'll still be awful. So the best case scenario, for me, is borderline unbearable. And you want to make it worse./ I'm not—/ Both of you. You and her. It doesn't matter who's at fault./ Doesn't matter to you./ Do you really want your funeral to be a clusterfuck?/ As long as there's booze./ It's on you, you know. If something goes wrong, it's not my fault./ I don't care. I'm not going to be there./ Then why does it matter if she comes?/ Because I refuse to let her win./ She's not trying to win. She's trying to . . ./ What?/ Get closure. Like everyone else./ She has it. She got it when we divorced. She got it when I stopped taking her calls./ She still cares about you./ No, she doesn't./ Just because she doesn't like you doesn't mean she doesn't care.

What does that mean?/ He can't stop you from coming, but he doesn't want you there./ I don't . . . What's that beeping?/ I don't know./ Are you still in the hospital?/ I'm down the hall./ From his room?/ Yeah./ Go home. It's late./ I'm aware./ You must be tired./ You have no idea./ Did you get any sleep last night?/ About four hours./ Are the pills helping?/ Yes and no. It's hard to say./ How long are you supposed to take them?/ As long as I want. As long as it takes./ How do you know if they're working?/ Can we talk about Dad?/ I'm not really sure what to tell you./ Tell me you're not going to come./ Sweetie . . ./ He's not calling Freddy./ So?/ He thinks you're not invited./ I don't care./ Well, *he* cares, and I care, and I don't want—/ You don't want an incident./ I don't want you there./ Yes, you do./ Of course I do. But I'm not the only one going. And if Dad doesn't want you there, and his family doesn't want you there, then I don't want you there either./ Why?/ I told you why./ You can't handle a fight./ I can't handle a fight, I can't handle the possibility of a fight, and I can't handle . . . Why do you think I'm taking the pills?/ I know./ Why do you think I'm . . ./ I know, Sweetie. I know.

Well, that's a relief./ No kidding./ Are you gonna head home?/ After I tell my dad./ Are you okay?/ Yeah. Not really. I don't know./ Give yourself a hug for me./ Okay./ And a kiss./ How's that going to work?/ I don't know. Kiss your hand or something./ Okay./ I miss you./ I know, buddy. I miss you too./ I wish I could help./ You *are* helping. Just by existing./ Smooch./ Double smooch./ I want to gobble you up./ Sounds painful./ And cuddle you. Cuddle, first. Gobble, second./ You're cute./ You're cuter./ It's not a competition./ I know. But if it was, I would win./ Probably./ Triple smooch./ Quadruple smooch./ BJ.

Really?/ Really./ She's not coming./ Nope./ She said that./ Yep./ She actually gave in./ I convinced her./ Unbelievable./ I guess I'm persuasive./ I didn't know she had it in her./ Apparently, she does. Can I leave now?/ What do you make of all this?/ I don't really care anymore./ Did she want to come?/

Of course./ I mean, really./ She *really* wanted to come./ Not out of.../ Malice? Spite? Boredom? No. She genuinely wanted to come. Any normal person would./ Well.../ In any case, it's over. So let's move on./ You got somewhere to be?/ Yeah. At home with my girlfriend./ Tell her I say hi./ Will do./ It wouldn't.../ What?/ It wouldn't be the end of the world if she came./ Natalie?/ Ruth./ You're kidding./ It wouldn't be the *end* of the world./ I'm not calling her again./ You don't have to. I'm just saying./ You want her to come./ I wouldn't *mind* if she came. "Want" might be a bit strong./ I can't fucking believe this.

So now he *wants* me to come?/ That's what he said./ Why?/ Fuck if I know. The man's insane./ What did he say?/ He said he "wouldn't mind" if you came./ He wouldn't *mind*? How nice of him./ So what should I tell him?/ Tell him to go fiddle himself./ Fiddle?/ Improvise, Max./ Should I tell him you're coming?/ No./ What? Why?/ He doesn't want me to come. He's made that perfectly clear./ Are you deaf? He changed his mind./ He didn't change a thing. You laid on the guilt, and he eventually caved. He agreed just to shut you up./ I swear that's not true. If you were here, you'd—/ Put him on the phone then./ I'm out of the room./ Go back to the room, and put him on the phone./ I doubt he wants to talk to you./ He wants me to come, but he doesn't want to talk to me?/ He doesn't *want* you to come./ He "wouldn't mind."/ Right./ Well, screw him./ *I* want you to come./ I want an apology./ From me?/ From him./ Not gonna happen./ Then I guess I'm not coming./ Jesus Christ./ He doesn't want me there, his family doesn't want me there, and I don't want to go where I'm not wanted./ He *does* want you there. He's just stubborn./ Well, so am I./ I can't fucking believe this./ It's just a funeral, Sweetie. Get some perspective.

Unbelievable./ I know./ That *person* is unbelievable./ I'm aware./ Who the hell does she think she is?/ I asked several times./ The mother of my only child won't come to my funeral./ Yep./ My wife of eighteen years./ Ex-wife./ Get her on the phone./ Seriously?/ Get her on the phone!/ It's been ten years./ Now!/

Okay, Jesus . . ./ Is it ringing?/ Yeah. Hold on./ Wait. Never mind. Hang up./ What?/ Hang up. I changed my mind./ Are you—/ Quickly!/ Voice mail./ Don't leave a message./ Wasn't going to./ God, that was close./ She said she had a dinner thing./ Dinner thing? With who?/ Does it matter?/ That guy? The real estate douche?/ They broke up a while ago./ Oh. Good. Him with her, or her with him?/ Her with him. She caught him cheating I think./ Asshole./ Yep./ Who's she seeing now?/ No idea./ But she's seeing *someone*./ I have no idea. I don't talk to her that much. And when I do, it's not about . . ./ Who she's banging./ Ugh. Jesus./ Hey, we're all adults here./ Not when it comes to that./ Speaking of banging, how's Melanie?/ Natalie./ Right. Natalie./ Natalie's wonderful. Thanks for asking./ What's she doing these days?/ Calming me down./ Huh?/ Nothing./ I can't believe I almost called her./ Natalie?/ Ruth./ Your idea, not mine./ It's *your* job to talk me out my ideas./ It's really more of a hobby than a job—/ Don't tell her I tried to call. Her ego is fat enough./ Do you want to try again later?/ No way. I refuse to talk to that—/ Stop calling her "person." I know what that means./ If she doesn't want to come, screw her. That's her problem./ I'd like her to come./ Then that's your problem./ Thanks, Dad./ I'm just so . . ./ What?/ I'm just so sick of this./ I know how you feel./ Fuck it. Let her do what she wants. If she wants to come, great. If she doesn't, also great. I don't care anymore./ So I can invite her?/ No, of course not./ But I can tell her to come./ No!/ What can I tell her then?/ Tell her she's . . . I don't know. Tell her what you want./ I'll ask her to come for me. Sans invitation./ No./ No, what?/ Ask her to come for me./ All right./ *Tell her* to come for me. I'm sick of all this asking. Tell her if she doesn't come to my funeral, I'll—/ Huff, and puff, and blow her house down?/ Don't get smart with me./ Relax. I'll ask again./ Tell. Not ask./ You're in no position to be giving orders, you know./ I'm in the best position. Giving orders is all I can do.

What is it? I'm out with Bob./ Who?/ Bob. My dinner . . . companion./ Dad wants you to come./ Mother of God./ That's what *I* said./ Officially, he wants me to come? Like an invitation?/

More like an order./ Well, he should've thought about that before he—/ Mom. Please. Just say yes, so I can go home./ I'm not just going to say yes. After what he put me through?/ Tonight?/ Every night./ You haven't seen him in—/ Every night we were married. Every day. Every hour—/ Give me a break./ Tonight's just another example./ He's not the only guilty party, you know./ And he's not the only innocent party either./ I understand that./ Does *he* understand that?/ Yes. Which is why he wants you to come./ He wants me to come because I *don't* want to come. It's a power play, and he knows it./ I swear to you, it's not. If you were here, you would see it./ See what?/ His . . . I don't know . . . vulnerability. It's in his voice. His eyes. It's written all over him./ Of course it is. He's dying. That's what happens when you—/ Hey!/ I'm not saying it to be mean; I'm saying it because it's true. He has no control over his life, so he's exercising what little he has over his death./ Wouldn't you?/ I probably would. But that doesn't make it any less manipulative. If he were well, this wouldn't be an issue./ If he were well, there wouldn't be a funeral./ Sweetie . . . Look. If I go, I'm going for you./ Whatever gets you through the eulogy./ He wants me to give a eulogy?!/ I'm kidding./ Oh. Thank God. Jesus . . ./ So we're agreed?/ On one condition./ Shit./ I want an apology./ I'm sorry./ From him./ He already apologized./ When?/ When he asked you to come. That's as close to an apology as you're going to get./ Fine. Do you have a caterer yet?/ No, not yet./ I can give you some names./ I'll forward them to Freddy. He's arranging everything./ Where's it being held?/ Dad's still alive, you know./ I know. I'm just . . ./ It's all right. I'll keep you posted as things develop./ Let me know if I can help./ I will. It'll probably be a small service. Friends and family./ Max would like that./ Yeah. I'll let you get back to your date./ Oh, don't worry. Bob's not going anywhere./ Yeah./ Sorry. Bad choice of words./ Don't worry about it./ I love you, Sweetie. You know that right?/ Uh huh./ We're doing our best, your dad and me. It might not seem like it, but we are./ So am I./ I know you are./ Yeah. Well . . . I should really get going./ Let me know what he says./ I think we both know what he'll say./ Something "Maxy." Followed by a grumble./ You're definitely coming? You won't change your mind?/ As long as he doesn't change his./ Even if he does .../ Sweetie. I'm coming. Tell Max to wear something nice.

Faces

<u>First Face</u>
People say I'm
<u>Second Face</u>
      two-faced
<u>Third Face</u>
              but they're wrong.
<u>Fourth Face</u>
I have more than two.
<u>Fifth Face</u>
I have three.
<u>Sixth Face</u>

<u>Trusting Face</u>
I have no reason to doubt people
<u>Suspicious Face</u>
      other than the following:

<u>Blank Face</u>
There's more to you than meets the eye.
<u>Animated Face</u>
There's less.

<u>Social Face</u>
I'm happy to see people
<u>Envious Face</u>
      in pain.
<u>Insecure Face</u>
      if people are happy to see me.
<u>Apprehensive Face</u>
      from a distance.

<u>Parasitic Face</u>
>who are happier than I am.
<u>Masochistic Face</u>
>who are happier than I am.

<u>Misanthropic Face</u>
People are evil and stupid
<u>Humanistic Face</u>
>sometimes.

<u>Solipsistic Face</u>
Neighbours do not exist
<u>Friendly Face</u>
>and are tolerable
<u>Unfriendly Face</u>
>>until they move in
<u>Violent Face</u>
>>>without asking.

<u>Mathematical Face</u>
Equations can be balanced
<u>Fascist Face</u>
>when anomalies are extinct.

<u>Religious Face</u>
God is
<u>Agnostic Face</u>
>problematic.
<u>Atheistic Face</u>
>absent.
<u>Gnostic Face</u>
>an asshole.

<u>Saintly Face</u>
Love ~~is~~
<u>Theoretical Face</u>
>can be patient and kind.

Ideal Face
>should be patient and kind.

Grounded Face
>should be a lot of things.

Conversational Face
You speak first.
Adversarial Face
.tsrif kaeps uoY

Faithful Face
I will always love you
Responsible Face
>if the price is right
Modern Face
>>and you do not age.

Timeless Face
I
Past Face
>was bad.
Present Face
>am bad.
Future Face
>will be better.
Future Perfect Progressive Face
>would have been better
Hypothetical Face
>>if not for
Regretful Face
>>>my timeless face.

One Face
You never
Another Face
You never

<u>One Face (continued)</u>
>let me finish.
<u>Another Face (continued)</u>
>let me start.
<u>One Face (concluded)</u>
>say what you mean.
<u>Another Face (concluded)</u>
>mean what you say.

<u>Translucent Face</u>
She *I* loves *love* me. *her.*
<u>Transparent Face</u>
She *I* loves *love* me not. *her not.*
<u>Brave Face</u>
We love each other
<u>Braver Face</u>
>not.

<u>Romantic Face</u>
Love is an illusion worth believing
<u>Practical Face</u>
>a reasonable fetish
<u>Nihilistic Face</u>
>>but . . .

<u>Damaged Face</u>
Good art opens old wounds.
<u>Cathartic Face</u>
Great art opens new ones.
<u>Pragmatic Face</u>
But no one reads anymore
<u>Healed Face</u>
>so we must be intact.

<u>Futile Face</u>
I am writing this because

<u>Stubborn Face</u>
    no one will read it
<u>Absurd Face</u>
                and if I don't write it
<u>Optimistic Face</u>
                        someone else will
<u>Pessimistic Face</u>
                            or they won't.

<u>Redundant Face</u>
I'm writing this because
<u>Exhausted Face</u>
    [insert text].

<u>Initial Face</u>
Happy.
<u>Mortal Face</u>
Sad.
<u>Final Face</u>
Happy.

<u>Sad Face</u>
Life is a joke
<u>Happy Face</u>
    but a funny joke.

OKCupid for Dummies

Rupert Pumpkin
filmgasmmmm.blogspot.com
Posted: 1:26AM, 08/26/2014

Step One: Upload pics.

Without pics, your profile is worthless. I don't care if you're Barack Hussein Obama. Without pics, you're just another stalker-psycho-serial-rapist.

But be careful which pics you choose. They're the first thing people see. You want to be honest yet mysterious, flashy yet subtle, confident yet humble.

No shots in front of cars. I don't care how "nice" you think they are.

No shots with your bros or anyone better-looking.

No selfies. (That goes without saying.) Especially selfies in front of a mirror.

And please, dress like a human. No one wants to see your photoshopped chest and/or your favourite Yankees hat. The chest says you're a douche; the hat says you're a tool. A tool with something to hide. (Especially if you're a Yankees fan.)

And avoid posing. Posing is for posers. Candid shots are great, even if they're staged. They make you seem less manufactured, less paint-by-numbers. You'll also seem less eager to impress.

Avoid tourist shots, as well. Especially goofy ones. Leaning on the Tower of Piza. Picking the nose of a giant Buddha. Pretending to dive into the Grand Canyon. None of this is original or impressive. It just showcases your reliance on clichés, your inability to live in the moment, and your willingness to commodify your experiences. Stop taking pictures for five fucking minutes and live your life.

When in doubt, use female profiles as a guide. If the girls you like post charming, G-rated pics, with lots of sunsets and daffodils, post similar pics yourself.

Take BlahBlah, for example. (Your hypothetical cyber-crush.) Let's say one of her pics shows her reading a Virginia Woolf novel with a cup of tea in her hand. Without reading a word of her profile, you can tell that she's smart, probably well-read, possibly an English (or Women's Studies) major, and that she might prefer tea to coffee.

Take notes, and calibrate your profile accordingly.

Step Two: Fill out your "I'm looking for" section.

Be honest (with yourself as well as others) but not too honest.

If you like women, say you like women. If you like men, say you like men. If you like everyone, say you like everyone. But only if you really mean it. Only if it's what you're *looking for*. If you're somewhat bi-curious but mostly straight, you might want to round off the decimals, for the sake of convenience.

Remember: this is a performance, not a confession. Tell us what you like, not what you secretly like, or what you think you might like if you just got dumped and you were drunk and a smokin hot trans chick walked into the bar and started flirting with you. Don't tell us that. Even if your dick moved a little when she touched your leg and you realized four drinks later that she was actually hotter than your ex in a lot of ways and you might be able to ignore her nether regions if you turn off the lights and close your eyes and keep your hands out of the area. Even then, don't tell us. Just tell us what you're looking for.

In terms of "ages," be realistic. If you're 45 and you want to bang a teenager, get a hooker. If you're a teenager and you want to bang a 45-year-old, get a therapist.

In other words, aim for folks your own age. For guys, the rule seems to be minus five years/plus two. (For girls, vice versa.) If you're a 23-year-old guy, you can date an 18-year-old girl, a 25-year-old girl, and anything in between. Straying beyond those parameters is ill-advised, at best. (And illegal, at worst.)

"Status" depends on your code of ethics. If you're a Puritan, who only wants to date single people, check "Must be single," but consider all the open relationship fallout you'll be missing.

The last category (what you're looking for) is the trickiest. Most guys don't join OKC to meet "new friends," unless they're anti-social or insane, and even if "casual sex" is high on your list of priorities, you're safer checking "long-term dating" and/or "short-term dating." Most girls—BlahBlah included—are looking to date, not just fuck. Otherwise, they'd be on Tinder.

Step Three: List your favourite films and books.

Everyone (I repeat: everyone) likes films. I have not met a human being, dead or alive, who does not. Therefore, include a short list ASAP to let people know you're from Earth: a couple of recent Oscar-winners, to show you have a heart, a classic or two, to show you have a brain, and one guilty pleasure (preferably a comedy, like *Bananas* or *Midnight in Paris*), to show you have a personality. You can deduce a lot about someone by their taste in films, so choose wisely.

If, like me, you're a huge film geek, feel free to include a longer list, but confine your list to films, not directors. Aside from Tarantino and Spielberg, normal people don't know directors. If you want to meet a fellow film geek with whom you can produce film geek kids who can star in your geeky films about film geeks, go ahead and list your favourite directors. Otherwise, stick to films. And be careful about listing anything by Woody Allen. These days, he's not exactly a safe choice . . . But more on that later.

Don't worry too much about books. These days, people just want to make sure you can read. Include a few obvious ones like *Harry Potter and the Chamber of Egrets,* and call it a day. (Remember: there's a fine line between literate and geeky. Cross it at your own risk.)

And take your cues from BlahBlah. If she lists *The Complete Works of Simone de Beauvoir* in her favourite books but neglects the

TV section entirely, you might want to think twice before including *Entourage* and *Californication* in yours.

Step Four: Fill out your details.

Be honest about your ethnicity, your height, your diet, your education, your orientation, and anything else that will come out eventually.

In the other sections, use your judgment. Most girls, for instance, prefer guys who drink socially but don't smoke. (Cigarettes, I mean, not weed. Cigarettes: no. Weed: maybe. It depends on the girl.)

"Religion" is a nightmare. Leave it blank, and save yourself the headache.

"Sign" is a joke. By filling it out, you legitimize it. Don't be a moron.

If, like most people, you're not too psyched about your job, feel free to input something vague, like "freelance consultant." If you're unemployed, either leave it blank or write "student." (We're all students in one sense or another . . .)

"Income" is another minefield. Broke = loser. Middle class = bore. Rich = target. Skip this section, for all the obvious reasons.

"Offspring" and "pets" are touchy subjects as well. 'Tis best to leave them blank, but if you feel compelled to write something, keep it sugar-coated. If you like torturing cats and/or eating dogs, keep that shit to yourself. (Same goes for children.)

Step Five: Write your self-summary.

Be concise. Be cool. Be casual.

Don't waste space with clichés like "It's so hard to sum up myself in a paragraph." We all know how awkward this is. There's no point in pointing it out.

And don't try to sum yourself up in a paragraph. Your profile is a marketing tool, not an autobiography. Dignity goes out the window the moment you sign in, as does intellectual rigor.

Keep it real. Keep it short. And always leave them wanting more. You need to intrigue without offending, beguile without overwhelming.

So be yourself, but be generic. The more you reveal, the more you concede. (One girl stopped talking to me because she saw *South Park* in my list of TV shows.)

Never lie, but never tell the truth (with a capital t). No one, including yourself, wants to hear that. As Baby Jesus once said, "Diplomacy is paramount."

Feel free to equivocate, embellish, exaggerate. But don't say you're a rock climber if you're afraid of heights. (I tried that one myself.)

Think of your profile as a resume, your first date as an interview. You want to be as professional as possible, without being stiff: a well-oiled machine with a personality.

And always, always, always present your "best self." If you're a laid-back guy, say it, but make sure you add something about your strong work ethic (even if it doesn't exist). Otherwise, she'll think you're a lazy meth-head. Laid-back: good. Meth-head: bad.

If you like reading and/or exercising, put that shit near the front. (Reading means you have a brain; exercising means you have a body. Most guys think reading is stupid, which is why girls think most guys are stupid. Which is why guys who read get laid.) If you like travelling and/or meeting new people, good for you. Who the hell doesn't? Put that shit near the end. If you like long walks on the beach, put that shit in your diary. If you like video games, delete your account. You're hopeless.

Sign off with an invitation. Something along the lines of "If you think we would get along, don't be shy. Say hi." It gives them an opening, and it makes you look friendly/accessible.

Remember: most guys interact with girls via threats or avoidance. (Sad but true. Our gender needs help.) Find the balance between macho douche and wimpy nerd. There are a lot of both on OKC, and it's your job not to be one of them. (Granted, the d-bags probably outnumber the nerds 10-1, but nerds can be just as annoying.) Therefore, avoid saying/doing anything that you wouldn't want said/done to your sister, your mom, or your girlfriend—assuming you'll someday find one. Avoid hipster-esque phrases like "too corporate" or "too mainstream" and hippie-esque clichés like "finding myself," "being present," and "embracing life." You sound unemployable, not to mention moronic.

There's a middle-ground between asshole strutting and pretentious self-fellating. My friend (who shall remain nameless (and who isn't really my friend (but don't tell him that))) is a part-time grad student, part-time musician. As well as—according to his OKC profile—a "part-time chef, a part-time mountaineer, and a full-time life-lover." Last week, he showed me his self-summary: "Whad up, Fellow Humans. I'm the co-founder/co-leader of a post-progressive folk band called Within-Time-Ness. Contrary to popular opinion, we deny our ontological status as a "band" (with a lower-case b) and problematize any praxis of aporetic discourse regarding the agency of our text or the text of our agency. Our debut album, 'Performative Blues,' (which is now available on cassette and vinyl) includes such songs as Deconstructing My Loneliness, You Make Me Feel So Phallic, Liminal Lovin', My Broken Logocentric Heart, Ain't No Marxist Like You, Howlin' Your Sound-Image, She's So Meta, Baby I Need Your Otherness, and our breakout single Nothin' But a Signifier." (As you might suspect, he's a fan of Derrida. But I doubt Derrida would've been a fan of him.)

Step Six: Leave the following sections blank.

What I'm doing with my life
I'm really good at
The most private thing I'm willing to admit
You should message me if

Step Seven: Fill out the others. (But only if you have something clever to say.)

For example, under *I spend a lot of time thinking about* I wrote "how much time I waste when I think about how much time I waste."

Clever, right? Any answer that isn't ironic, self-deprecating, or a combination of the two is a bad answer. (Most guys write stuff like "my career," "my homies," and/or "the mysteries of the universe." Eye roll. Barf.)

Step Eight: Answer personality questions.

A hundred or so should suffice. Just enough to get a sense of who you are and what you like. The more you answer, the more accurate your matches will be.

On the other hand, the more you answer, the more you reveal. So don't answer 1000. (I'm not even sure if there are 1000 . . .)

And don't answer the ones that make you uncomfortable. If you have a super-duper-top-secret foot fetish, don't answer the foot fetish question. Same goes for questions about golden showers, anal beads, and anything involving tentacles. (See Japanese porn for more details . . .)

That said, if you want to know how BlahBlah feels about foot fetishes—not to mention golden showers, anal beads, and anything involving tentacles—you'll have to answer the question as well. For better or worse, OKC knowledge is reciprocal.

P.S. For the masturbation question, go with "a few times a week." Any more and you'll look like a pervert. Any less and you'll look like a monk.

Step Nine: Send a message.

Don't just say "Hi" or "You're cute." Girls don't want their cuteness assessed by strangers, especially by lazy strangers who can't be bothered to write more than a one- or two-word message.

Ask a question. A harmless question that will intrigue without offending. Something like, "If you could live anywhere in Europe, where would it be?" It's easy to answer, fun to answer, and easy to ask again. In short, a great conversation-starter.

Once you settle on a safe, universally-appealing question, copy and paste it into every message you send. (This may sound heartless, but you'll save a lot of time. Besides, girls aren't looking for a sonnet. They just want an opening that doesn't sound like a pick-up line or a death threat.)

However (and whoever) you message, try not to get invested. I know it's hard, especially when you find a genuine cyber-crush—a BlahBlah—but, trust me, there are better ways to spend your tears. If they don't respond, move on to someone who will.

And set a browsing limit. 10 seconds per profile is reasonable. 30 is the absolute max. Once you check out their head shots, body shots, compatibility ratings, and self-summary, send your message and click on the next profile. I can send over ten messages a minute, once I get into a rhythm.

I have a checklist: Are they attractive? Are they compatible? Are they interesting? Are they sane? If I can answer Yes (or Probably) to at least three out of four, I send a message. Always leave room for red herrings: not everyone is photogenic, OKC's matching system is known to miscalculate, some folks are only interesting in person, and—last but not least—sanity is relative.

Let's say you message BlahBlah, asking your template Europe question, and she responds, "Amsterdam." Feel free to tell her about a trip to Amsterdam you may have taken. You could mention the Anne Frank house, the Van Gogh Museum, and your weed-smoking adventures in the Red Light District.

BlahBlah might ask if you hooked up with any prostitutes while you were there. Categorically deny, even if you have to lie. Chances are, she wouldn't approve. But keep it casual. Say something like, "No lol Of course not," so you don't look suspicious. (You can always add a well-considered follow-up, expressing your thoughts on prostitution, if you feel so inclined.)

Once you've exchanged a couple of messages, feel free to ask her out. (For coffee or drinks, not a gang bang. Unless under *I'm looking for* she explicitly wrote, "a gang bang." In which case, ask away.)

"You seem pretty cool. Would you like to hang out sometime?" usually works for me. If she says yes, suggest a coffee date. Always pick the same time and place, to remove unwanted variables. The afternoon, if you're in your 20s; the evening, if you're not. A coffee shop close to home and, if possible, a park. That way, you can take a stroll if it's a nice day, and if things go really well, you're just a few minutes away from your bedroom!

(Speaking of which, check out her personality questions to see where she stands on issues like sex on a first date, accidental pregnancies/abortions, STIs, and anything else that might be a deal-breaker. If, for example, you're a kinky dink and she's a clean-cut Carol, it's better to know sooner rather than later . . .)

But keep in mind: 99 percent of the time, things will not work out. If you send 100 messages, maybe 20 people will respond—if you're lucky. Unless you're rich or bizarrely handsome, you're more likely to receive 15 (or even 10) responses. Of those 15, maybe half will reply more than once, and only half of *them* will agree to meet you in person. Of the three remaining, two will actually show up, and only one will want to see you more than once. (Incidentally, "more than once" does not imply anything more than twice.)

Sounds bleak, right? But what's the alternative? Another night at the bar? Another house party? Do the numbers on a house party. How many people can fit in a house? 30? Maybe 40? Of those 40, maybe 10 will be attractive. And just because they're attractive doesn't mean they're single. And just because they're single doesn't mean they're looking. And just because they're looking doesn't mean they're looking for you.

Sometimes you'll wish people *didn't* reply to your messages. A few months ago, for instance, I found myself in an unprovoked argument with someone who, for propriety's sake, shall remain nameless. "Hey M.," I wrote, "you seem to be both intelligent and down-to-earth, and, in my experience, that's a pretty rare combination. If you could live anywhere in Europe where would it be?" "I'll try to be witty," she replied. "Most people aren't intelligent nor down-to-earth. If they're one, they're the other. And since your name states you're one, you probably aren't the other." (FYI: my username includes the word "witty.") Then she added, in a separate message, "Lots of love! M." Naturally, I was pissed, so I wrote back: "I'll try to be more witty, which shouldn't be very hard in this case. First, you misused the word 'nor.' Second, read a psychology textbook. Third, my username is ironic. Fourth, your third and fourth sentences contradict each other. (If you're going to criticize people, you should probably make sure that your criticism makes sense.) Fifth, based on how quickly you reached your judgment and how you went out of your way to share it with me, you clearly are neither intelligent NOR down-to-earth, and I'm sorry I misjudged you." Then I waited a few minutes and added, "Lots of love! Witty [the rest of my username]" Granted, I was probably a bit harsh, but so was she. And I'm entitled to defend myself.

Which is a long way of saying, not all messages will be pleasant. Some will be nasty; some will be downright silly. One girl (let's call her Shouty) ended every sentence, no matter how mundane, with an exclamation mark: "Hey! My weekend was okay! I went grocery shopping and cleaned my apartment! How was yours?!?!" Another girl, who I've nicknamed Winky, used emoticons instead of punctuation: "hi there ;) you seem interesting :p send a dick pic :)" And Abby, as I've come to call her, seemed allergic to actual words: "lol idk. meh. w/e ... brb ... sry i g2g. ttyl ... ps u dtf tmrw?" Part of me wanted to meet these people just to see what they were like in person—to see if they spoke in abbreviations or smiled in symbols. But these are minor offences compared to the full-frontal assaults of people like M.

I have a not-too-original theory that the internet is just an enabling mechanism for asshole-ish behavior. If I met M. at a party, for instance, and gave her the same "intelligent and down-to-earth" compliment, she would never say what she said. Not to my face, at least. The online barrier of anonymity not only protects her but dehumanizes me, allowing her to get away with insults that, in any other context, would be completely unacceptable. And the sad thing is, she's probably a decent person. In "real life," she's probably polite and thoughtful and empathetic, but online she's a dick. Why? Because there are no apparent consequences for her actions. She can say whatever she wants—no matter how moronic or offensive—without fear of retribution, because, in a sense, I'm not a real person; I'm just a collection of data and megapixels. The same can obviously be said about guys who think it's okay to greet women online by listing all the ways they'd like to fuck them. In their day-to-day lives, such reptilian tools are probably afraid to make eye contact with women, but the online forum enables them to get away with obscene levels of dickishness. The point, however, is universal. Etiquette is etiquette, regardless of gender, and a dick with a vagina is no better than a dick with a dick.

Even I'm guilty of this kind of duplicity. My outer self, my public persona, is much more patient, civil, and polite than the person who tumbles around in my head, breaking things. Out of pragmatism I try to be my "best self" with others and restrict my "real self" to late night appearances, when everyone else has gone to bed.

But that's the way we've always been. Jekylls hide their Hydes; Hydes hide their Jekylls. Hitler was right: If you're pretty on the outside, you're probably ugly on the inside. (Jk. Hitler didn't say that. It was Stalin.) The reverse is true, as well: if you're ugly on the outside, you're probably pretty on the inside. Too bad we can only see what we prioritize. The skin-deep beauty. The social shell.

Step Ten: Brainstorm conversation topics.

If you have a bad memory, write them on the back of a business card, and stick it in your wallet. You can always refer to it when you go to the bathroom. But NEVER pull it out in front of BlahBlah. You. Will. Look. Insane.

Cater the topics to your date's interests, but focus on areas of common ground. If she likes Woody Allen films, and you like Woody Allen films, write down "Woody Allen films." (But don't assume that she *still* likes them. Or that you both like the same ones. Opinions change, and people don't always update their profiles . . .)

Once you get to know her, feel free to explore more interesting topics. I sometimes share my People I Don't Necessarily Want Dead But Wouldn't Feel Bad If They Died list. (Which includes several celebrities and politicians, as well as a few classmates from high school.) Tailor your list to your audience, and be sure to mention the least controversial choices (like Justin Bieber) up front.

Last year, this experiment back-fired big time, when I included the mayor on my list. My date didn't seem to mind at the time, but after we parted ways I got a call from the cops, asking if I was politically active, if I harbored any ill-will towards my current municipal representatives, and if I had ever been involved in a terrorist organization. I replied, "No," "No," and "Define 'terrorist.'" Things went downhill from there . . . (It wasn't all bad though. A few months later, I turned our date into a short film!)

Step Eleven (A): Manage your nervous breakdown.

Let's say BlahBlah doesn't show up.
    Whatever you do, don't send a half-dozen angry messages. I know you may want to, but don't. That shit's written in ink, and it's easy to share with the world. Whatever rage you feel—justly or unjustly—take it out on a pillow or a trash can.

Step Eleven (B): Manage your nerves.

Let's say BlahBlah *does* show up.
    Whatever you do, don't get too excited. Just be yourself, and take things sentence-by-sentence. If you pass a weird sign, for instance, don't be afraid to stop and speculate about its meaning.

When I went out with the girl who foiled my scheme to assassinate the mayor, we passed a theatre showing a student production called *Nobodies: A Play About Everyday Heroes*. "Nobodies," she mumbled, looking up at the sign. "Sounds like No Buddies, if you say it quickly." "Or No Bodies," I replied, "if you say it slowly." "Or Nobo Dies, if you say it weirdly." Who was Nobo, we wondered, and why did he die? Did he have no buddies? No body? We knew what it meant to have no buddies, but what would it mean to have no body? Did a brain in a jar count as a body? Probably not. What if you added arms and legs to the jar and drew a smiley face? At what point, in other words, did body parts end and bodies begin? These are the kinds of things you discuss on a first date. They mean nothing and lead nowhere, but they sure are fun.

Don't assume she's into you, but don't assume she's not. Just because she seems uncomfortable doesn't mean she's not having fun. But just because she's having fun doesn't mean she likes you. (And just because *you're* having fun doesn't mean *she's* having fun.)

Conversation-wise, you'll never know where the landmines are until you step on one. At that point just collect your limbs and get the hell out of there.

Step Twelve: Avoid stepping on the same landmine twice.

If, for instance, you find yourself in an argument with BlahBlah about Woody Allen's alleged pedophilia, end it ASAP. You may feel the urge to raise your voice and call her names, especially since her profile—which includes *Annie Hall* and *Vicky Christina Barcelona* (among others) in her Favourite Movies section—has led you to believe that she's a fan of Allen's work/character. You'll want to tear your teeth out, because she's a hypocrite, and you're a well-intentioned, compassionate human being who's just trying to make small talk and find common interests and who's now defending an alleged child molester for no particular reason. You'll repeat your point again and again, as if hearing it for a fourth time will finally convince her, and when she starts to challenge you, finding the holes in your argument (not to mention your Ghandi-like persona), you'll be too proud to admit defeat, to acknowledge your own hypocrisy, and you'll volunteer to end the date early.

If you're lucky, you'll find common ground, agree to disagree, and change the subject in time to salvage your relationship. Chances are, you won't. But miracles happen.

Step Thirteen: Follow up.

After you say adios, wait a few days to text her. (Don't call. Calling is so 20th Century.) If she doesn't reply within 24 hours, remain calm. It might be nothing. Send a follow-up text, just to confirm. If she doesn't respond to Text Number Two, take the hint: she ain't that into you. Let it/her go, and move on to someone who is.

If she does respond, ask her out again. (Regardless of how the first date went.)

Of course, there's no guarantee that the second date will be better. Let's say you go see the new Woody Allen film, *Magic in the Moonlight*. As you leave the theatre, and she tells you how much she liked it (despite the creepy *Whatever Works/Manhattan*-esque relationship between Colin Firth and Emma Stone) you'll smile and nod and suppress the urge to share your rant, which is now coiled in your brain like a sneeze, ready to spray at the slightest provocation. You'll try to steer the conversation away from *M in the M* (and away from Woody Allen in general), but before you can she suggests that *M in the M* may not have been as good as *Vicky Christina Barcelona* but was still better than *Manhattan*, not to mention *Midnight in Paris* and *Annie Hall*. And once you recover from your minor stroke, you sort out the questions snapping your neurons. How could she prefer *VCB* to *Manhattan*? Or *M in the M* to *Manhattan*? Or *M in the M* to *Midnight in P*? Or *M in the M* to *Annie H*? Or *VCB* to *Midnight in P*? Or *VCB* to *Annie H*?

You wonder (very sincerely) if you can respect someone who prefers the melodrama of *VCB* or the fifth-rate farce of *M in the M* to the infinite artistry of *Manhattan*. How could you, an aspiring filmmaker, date someone with such terrible taste? Imagine what she'll say when she sees one of your films. She'll think you're a hack, a poser, a fraud, and you'll think she's an ignorant, soulless moron, who wouldn't recognize good art if it fell on her head. (Which you secretly hope might happen, preferably in the form of a large marble sculpture.)

You try to imagine a future with BlahBlah. You picture arguments in the street, in the kitchen, in the bedroom. You chart the slow creep of resentment: the sighs, the rolling eyes, the silent treatments and loud debates. You watch minor become major, as pet-peeves morph into deal-breakers.

You try again to change the subject, but she asks for your thoughts on *M in the M*, and (for reasons that you are unable to explain to your therapist) you tell the truth. You ridicule the childish plot, the sentimental lighting, and the complete lack of chemistry between Colin Firth and Emma Stone. BlahBlah goes predictably, understandably quiet. But you don't stop there. (Why would you? You've already shot yourself in the foot; you might as well shoot the other foot too.) You defend your beloved *Manhattan*, expounding on its richness, celebrating its wise humor/humorous wisdom, but before you have a chance to recite your favourite lines, she waves a dismissive hand and says, "Ugh. It's sooooo overrated."

She goes on to list the virtues of *VCB*, citing the golden cinematography, the lush landscapes, and the Oscar-winning performance by Penelope Cruz—all of which is fine 'n dandy (to use one of BlahBlah's favourite expressions) but doesn't add up to a great film. Or even a decent film. Sure, it's okay by Hollywood standards, but the plot is absurd, the dialogue is cheesy, and the voiceover narration is nauseating. Not only is *VCB* not comparable to *Manhattan* (which, for the record, is clearly and obviously Allen's best film—period, end of story), but *VCB* isn't even in the Allen Top Ten. (Or, for that matter, the Top Twenty.)

Adding insult to injury, she lists a half-dozen Allen films that she prefers to *Manhattan*. You don't have enough patience to refute the absurd choices (like *Match Point*, *You Will Meet a Tall Dark Stranger*, and *To Rome with Love*) so you confine your counter-arguments to films that actually have merit: *Annie H* and *Midnight in P*. (Two classics, for sure, but not quite *Manhattan*.) She gives the usual arguments in favour of *Annie H*: it won more Oscars, invented a fashion style, etc. etc.

But *Annie H* is the easy choice. Like picking Beethoven's 5th or 9th Symphonies over the 7th. The 5th is the most accessible, the 9th is the most ambitious, but the 7th is the most subtle, the most mature, the most flawless. It doesn't try too hard, it isn't too flashy, and, unlike the 9th, it doesn't overstay its welcome. Same goes for Pink Floyd's *Wish You Were Here* compared to *Dark Side of the Moon* and *The Wall*. *Dark Side* is the album everyone loves first, followed by *The Wall*, which, like Beethoven's 9th, is a bit patchy in spots, not to mention longwinded, but *Wish You Were Here* is the underappreciated middle child. The perfect blend of ambition and refinement, subtlety and sublimity.

You don't explain any of this to her, because you don't want to sound like more of a douche-nerd than you already do, but you think it, again and again, a half-hour later, on the subway ride home. Alone.

This time, you part ways abruptly, on not-so-good terms. You don't even get a hug. (In a sense, hugs are worse than slaps. They offer a sample of bodily contact, but not too much, and not for too long. Just enough for you to know what you're missing.)

When you get home, you go through the usual motions: resenting her, wanting her, resenting while wanting, wanting while resenting. You wonder why you even like her. She's attractive, yes, but so are a lot of people.

You wonder if these minor issues—*Manhattan*, pedophilia, etc.—are really so important. Maybe they're just defense mechanisms preventing you from becoming attached. Maybe you're just afraid of pain and loss, like everyone else. Isn't that why things didn't work out with Janet or Mary or Emma or Claire? (Not to mention Julia, Monica, and Stacy?) Isn't that why you fucked things up with BlahBlah too? Because deep down you're determined to die alone, like your mother always said?

Suddenly, you realize you've smoked too much weed. You put your bong back on the table, push yourself off the couch and grab a glass of water from the kitchen. You try to forget about your exes and your mother, and you focus on BlahBlah instead.

You assume she won't want to see you again, which is just fine by you. She's arrogant, and opinionated, and abrasive, and judgmental. Who the hell would want to be with someone like that? (Yes, I'm aware of the irony.)

So why, you ask yourself, is she getting under your skin? Why are you so desperate to see her again, if you can't stand the sight of her? To maintain your OKC track record? To appease your ego? To reject her before she can reject you? To get a second second chance? To prove to her you're not a douche? To prove to *yourself* you're not a douche?

All of the above, plus the below:

You have nothing (and no one) better to do.

Which isn't as callous as it sounds. Using people—sexually, emotionally, financially—is standard operating procedure these days, at least in the early stages. As long as the use is consensual/mutual. As long as you're *both* using/being used.

You pick up your phone to text her an apology—maybe even a request for Date Number Three—but before you can type "Hey," you realize how desperate/weak you'll look, so you put the phone down and pick up your bong.

Over the next 48 hours, you look at her profile 12 times, reread your messages twice, replay Date Number One in your head three times, Date Number Two seven times, check your phone 26 times, start and stop and erase a text message 9 times, and wonder whether you'll ever see her again on a minute-by-minute basis.

After three full days of radio silence, you text a simple "Sorry about the other night" and wait eight-and-a-half hours (which feels like eight-and-a-half days) for BlahBlah to reply. When she does, she offers a one-line enigma: "annie hall is still better than manhattan."

You don't know how to respond. Is she joking? Is she trying to piss you off? Is she provoking another argument—this time, via text—or prompting a third date request?

You don't reply for 37 minutes, unsure of what to say or how to say it.

Finally, you pick up your phone and type "You're entitled to your opinion" but then erase it and write "How about we agree to disagree?" instead. You stare at the glowing letters, double-checking your syntax, spelling, and diction, like a paranoid ESL student. Just press SEND, you tell yourself.

Against its better judgment, your self obeys.

While you wait for her to respond, you check out her profile again, searching for clues that you might have missed, but after rereading her self-summary and a solid six pages of personal questions, you've learned nothing, and you feel even more helpless than before.

An hour passes, with no response, and you ask yourself, Why are you doing this?

The answer arrives like a punch in the chest: Because you like her. For some inexplicable reason, you actually like her. And she likes you. (At least, that's what you tell yourself.) So you wait. And wait. And wait.

Will BlahBlah reply?

Your guess is as good as mine.

Tune in tomorrow. Maybe we'll find out.

The Librarian

"History is a nightmare from which I am trying to awake."
—James Joyce, *Ulysses*

A sparsely decorated section of the local library. Across the back wall a long, absurdly tall shelf, half-filled with novels of dubious quality. A short desk with a burnt-out, dusty lamp and a wooden stool underneath. In the corner, an easy-chair surrounded by books and papers.

Steven, a twenty-something graduate student, is sorting novels from a cart beside the desk, placing them methodically on the shelves. Every few books, he lets out a sigh, then continues with his task.

Four days of grease have sorted his hair into wavy clumps, extending up, out, and sideways, as though designed by Frank Gehry. Whenever the frontal strands break rank, Steven tucks them to the side, concealing one section of his v-shaped hairline while revealing the other. The left is farther back than the right, but both seem to recede and thin, these days, by the hour.

His features below the skull are no more impressive. His limbs have stiffened and slimmed from neglect, along with his back, which looks more like a question mark with each passing lecture. The usual five o'clock shadow has crept up his neck and onto his sun-starved face, and his chest hair—which was once as carefully groomed as an 18th century shrub—has crested his collar bone and plunged, without warning, into the valleys of his neck.

His clothes, on the other hand, are typical of someone in the field. His button-up shirt is wrinkled and coffee-stained, as are his khakis, neither of which seem to fit his lanky frame. His sleeves are rolled; his buttons, half-undone; his pants, upheld by a belt with extra holes. Walking around campus, he assumes people think he is either a hobo or a PhD candidate, and he can never decide which label is more embarrassing.

Steven slides a final book onto the shelf and checks a list on the table. He stands back and examines his work, arms folded.

"Done the As . . ." He walks over to the cart. "Now the Bs."

A stunning brunette in a cocktail dress appears out of the section of the stacks where people rarely go. Her hair is poised; her skin, spotless. She walks like a runway model returning from a Mensa meeting: confident, elegant, yet sly, as though in on a joke that no one else gets. Both proud of her brain and aware of her beauty, she wears a posture to match her heels and a grin to go with her dress.

She approaches Steven casually, watching him work.

He doesn't seem to notice her presence. Or he notices but doesn't seem to care. Or he both notices *and* cares but doesn't want her to think so.

She considers each alternative, then sits in the easy-chair beside the pile of books in the corner. She crosses her legs, picks up a dusty, leather-bound tome, flips through it, then tosses it on the ground.

"Be careful with that," Steven says, as though for the hundredth time. "It's very old."

She picks it up and reads the cover. *"James Joyce: The Definitive Biography." Doesn't every biography think it's "definitive"?*

Before he can answer, Emma approaches, pushing a cart filled with books. Steven forces his lips, muscle by muscle, into an upward curve. With most human beings he can summon a smile with ease, but whenever Emma walks by, wearing her handstitched, moth-eaten sweater, his mouth seems to forget how to function.

"Where do you want these?" Emma asks, gathering her strawberry strands into a ponytail.

Steven points to the other cart. "Just there is fine."

She walks it over, then stands beside him in front of the shelf. They look from the shelf to the new cart, overflowing with books. He turns to her but looks away when she turns to him. He scratches his head. She looks down at her feet.

Unlike the Mensa model, Emma has looks and talent but lacks the will to use them. She is the kind of girl who still calls her parents, who writes thank you notes, who stares at the sidewalk instead of the sky. She never experiments with drugs or men. She never jaywalks. She obeys the laws of the world and the laws of her mind, even when she disagrees with them. She has worked hard to be humble, to be happy with low expectations, but she secretly longs to be shattered, to be picked up by the winds of fate and carried away, into the unknown. Her mother thinks she's a lion with the confidence of a cat, a cat with the ambition of a mouse. Her father thinks she's a mouse with the ambition of a lion. She thinks she's a mouse with the ambition of a mouse.

THUMM!

The Mensa model has dropped another book on the floor. Steven's head turns instantly, but Emma doesn't seem to notice the noise. She sees Steven glaring at the empty corner and asks, "What's wrong?"

"Nothing," he says, pretending to search for a book on the cart.

Emma looks again at the vacant corner. The Mensa model waves to her, smiling sardonically.

"Well," Emma says, "I should get back to it."

"Yeah. I should too."

"Drop by if you get bored."

She smiles and walks away. He watches her leave.

Once she's gone, he shakes his head and begins stocking the shelves with books from the new cart.

Well done, Romeo, says the Mensa model, flipping through another book.

(Like most people of sanity, Steven has voices in the back of his head, prattling on in times of stress or times of boredom. He doesn't "hear" voices, in the schizophrenic sense; nevertheless, he has accumulated, over the years, a series of influences, who continue to assault his consciousness, who have left their mark on his soul yet refuse to leave his mind. The Mensa model is one of them. A voice that continues to speak long after its source has been silenced.)

She wanders over to his desk. *So what's the plan? Seduce her in the stacks? I hear the history section is quite romantic after midnight.*

Steven keeps shelving.

Or would you rather just grab her and throw her down on the photocopier? I like the simplicity. Just make sure you don't press "print" this time.

She turns to gauge his reaction.

You could always leave love notes in the overdue books. That seemed to work for the last one.

Still no reaction.

I can't say I blame her for quitting. I'd quit too if I thought you were stalking me.

"I *am* working, you know."

Oh yes, the big important grad student, making the world a better place, one properly shelved book at a time.

"It's just a job."

I wonder if I'll still hear that when you're thirty.

"If you're still around when I'm thirty, I'll have bigger issues to deal with."

That, my friend, is entirely up to you. But between the two of us, I don't think I'm leaving any time soon.

Steven examines the list on the table, then folds his arms and inspects the shelves. His counterpart does the same, mockingly.

"Done the Bs . . ." he mutters.

Now the Cs.

Steven starts working again. Emma joins him with another cart full of books.

"That was fast."

"Yeah," Emma says, "I need to get out of here. I can't believe he made us do this on a Friday night."

"The man's evil."

She laughs. "Yeah. Well, if you need any help, just ask, okay?"

"Thanks. Will do."

She smiles and leaves.

She's a cutie. A real sweetie-pie.

"She has a boyfriend."

You're hopeless either way.

"Thanks, hun."

She approaches him coyly, as if trying to seduce him.

"What do you want?"

I'm her. You're you. Now what?

"Now nothing. You're in my way."

Yes, I am.

He glares at her, half-frustrated, half-afraid.

She disappears into the shadows of the stacks, only to return seconds later, pushing a cart filled with porn magazines and anatomy textbooks. Dildos of various shapes and sizes, colours and patterns, sprout out of the pile like a bouquet of thick rubber flowers.

"Jesus Christ," Steven mumbles, massaging his temples.

Hi, there, she says, imitating Emma's voice. *Where would you like these?*

"It's 10:30. I want to go home."

She flutters her eyes playfully. *Are you doing anything this weekend?*

"Okay, she would never act like that."

She picks up one of the anatomy textbooks and strokes the cover seductively.

Boy, you sure are good with books. She holds the book to her chest. *I think people who read are sexy.* She tosses the book back on the cart and walks toward him. *You know what I think is more sexy?* She pulls his collar, as if she were going to kiss him, then whispers in his ear, *Librarians.*

Steven rolls his eyes and sighs. She drops the act and releases him.

Now what's wrong with that picture?

"I'm not sure where to begin."

Librarians aren't sexy. People who read books aren't sexy. Therefore . . .

"I'm not sexy."

Bingo.

"Is that why you dumped me?" he asks, returning to work. "I wasn't sexy enough for you?"

You weren't sexy enough for someone.

Confused and annoyed, Steven watches her wander back to the easy-chair in the corner and sit down. She picks up a stack of papers lying on top of a book.

"*The Dark Side of Consciousness in* Ulysses: *Existential Motifs in Molly Bloom's Monologue.*" *Where would we be without it . . .*

"I got an A on that, by the way."

I'd expect nothing less.

She flips through it, giggling every few seconds. He tries to ignore her.

She reads a passage aloud: *"Joyce had a bookcase full of people—friends and family, rivals and enemies—whom he tried to impress. Those who believed he was destined for greatness, he tried to prove right; those who did not, he tried to prove wrong. Each day, he gazed up at his bookcase to remind himself where he came from and where he still had to go. Anyone who offered encouragement shined a warm, gentle light on his spirit, which the darkness of discouragement could never fully absorb. As his vision failed and his need for illumination increased, he placed his supporters on the top shelves and his detractors on the bottom, hoping the light of the former would wash away the dark of the latter. But over the years, as the bookcase grew both in volume and size, the ratio of supporters to detractors shrunk, forcing the light higher and higher until it was out of sight, and he was left blind and alone, battling ghosts in the darkness."*

She examines the paper, grinning enigmatically. *Why didn't he just light a candle?*

Steven doesn't respond.

And how do books shine a warm and gentle light? Did they have mushrooms in the 30s?

Steven keeps working.

Or are the books just supposed to be people? In which case, I think you're mixing your metaphors. People don't shine unless they're on fire.

Steven allows himself to smile, but doesn't let her see it.

She looks up from the essay. *Did you read the new Francis Duvall novel?*

His smile fades and his eyes close. "No."

It's really good. Won all the big awards.

"That's nice."

The Anderson Award, The Morrison Medal, The Pynchon Prize. The North-East 72nd Street Chinatown Grant—

"Good for him."

He's the next Joyce, a lot of people say. Except he can write poetry as well as fiction.

Steven takes a deep breath, trying to remain calm.

Twenty-six and already a prize-winning author. A prize-winning, bestselling, critically acclaimed—

"Do you mind?"

Oh, I'm sorry. I forgot to ask. How's your novel coming?

"I've been busy."

Ah, yes. Full of ideas and things to say, and not enough time to say them. She waits a moment to let the insult sink in, then lets loose the next arrow in her quiver: *Have you read Walter Bishop's new book?*

"Nope."

Emily Jordan's?

"Nein."

What about Joyce?

He turns to her, confused but intrigued.

Didn't you hear? They just published a new collection of his letters.

"I know," he says, turning back to the shelves. "It's over there."

She spots the book on the edge of the desk and reads the cover. *"The Letters of James Joyce: 1916-1923, Volume One." Compelling stuff, I'm sure.*

He opens his mouth to reply but stops himself.

It's funny, isn't it? He's been dead almost eighty years, and he's still publishing more than you.

Steven marches over, as if to attack her, then picks up one of the books on the desk and starts flipping through it. After a few seconds of searching, he stops, circles something and makes a note in the margin.

Should I even ask?

"An idea for my thesis."

Oh, yes. Your magnum opus. How's that coming?

"It's what I've been 'busy' with."

What's it on again?

"Haven't decided exactly."

What's it called?

"So far? 'Post-structural Linguistics in *Finnegans Wake*: A Psychoanalytic Perspective.'"

A bit vague, don't you think?

Steven ignores her.

Just what the world needs. Another book on Joyce.

She picks up a thick, hardcover copy of *Ulysses* from the pile in the corner, and, watching Steven, drops it on the floor. He doesn't flinch.

How many do you think are published every year? And how many do you think are actually read? By more than six people, I mean.

Steven keeps shelving, book after book.

Yours will be different though. You're doing a Freudian analysis of a book no one can understand. Why shouldn't you be optimistic?

Steven shelves a book with his left hand and gives her the finger with his right.

By the way, if you're worried about getting your novel out there, you might want to consider self-publishing. Of course, you probably won't have any more readers than you do now, but at least it'll be in print. Two or three copies, sitting on shelves. Waiting for someone like you to sort them out. Dust them off.

Steven stands in front of the shelves and examines the list.

Done the Cs?

"Now the Ds."

He starts working again. She grabs an old copy of *Finnegans Wake* from the pile, opens it and starts reading in a cartoonish Irish accent. *"O tell me all about Anna Livia."*

Steven sighs.

"I want to hear all about Anna Livia. Well, you know Anna Livia?"

"Yes, of course," Steven says, completely deadpan, "we all know Anna Livia. Tell me all. Tell me now."

"You'll die when you hear."

"I doubt it."

She closes the book and tosses it on the pile. *You're no fun today.*

"Am I fun any other day?"

She puts her hands on her hips and sizes him up. *Why are you doing this?*

He turns to her, surprised by her directness, her apparent sincerity. "Why am I doing what?"

Before she can answer, they hear Emma's approaching footsteps and the squeaky wheels of a cart.

"Don't worry," Emma says, as she moves into view. "Only one more after this." She parks the book-filled cart beside the others. "How's it coming?"

"Slowly."

"You want some help?"

"Uh . . ."

Yes.

"Sure," Steven says, looking from the Mensa model to Emma.

"Okay," Emma says, as she leaves, "I only have one more cart to catalogue and—"

Stop her.

"Wait," Steven says, extending an arm towards Emma.

She stops walking and turns. "Yeah?"

Steven looks to the Mensa model for guidance. She grins mischievously.

"Uh . . ."

Say what you want to say.

Steven looks back at Emma. "Nothing. Never mind."

"I'll be back soon."

She leaves. Steven watches her go.

You pussy.

"She has a boyfriend," Steven says, regaining his composure. "I'm not asking her out."

His counterpart scoffs. *When was the last time you went on a date? Please don't say it was with me.*

Steven doesn't respond.

When was the last time you showered?

She picks up another book from the pile, sighing. *What would Joyce say if he could see you now?* She looks up at him again, as if to double-check something. *Have you put on weight?*

Steven throws her a dirty look.

I remember when you used to sit on the couch after class, eating those chocolate chip cookies.

"Is that why you dumped me, I was a cookie monster?"

That was the tip of the iceberg.

"Why were you with me then?"

Can't remember.

"Why did you dump me?"

Oh, so many reasons.

"Was I too stupid? Too ugly? Too . . . average?"

You were too . . . everything.

"Then why were you with me?"

You're going to keep asking?

"Until I get an answer."

She sighs. *I was with you . . . so I could torture you. I'm Satan's twin sister. Pure evil. Happy?*

"Not particularly."

At least you'll have some new material for your novel.

"Great."

Am I in there somewhere?

"No."

Oh, I bet I am. I bet I'm all over it. I bet I give you writer's block.

"What the hell does that mean?"

You wouldn't know what to do with me. You never did.

He shoves a book onto the shelf, fuming. "I know what to do with you . . ."

Please. You have no idea. Just like your little girlfriend in there.

"She has a boyfriend."

Oh, yes, I'm sure that's what's stopping you.

He stands back from the shelves and picks up the list.

Done the Ds?

"Yeah."

Now the Es.

Emma enters with another cart full of books.

Right on cue.

"All right," Emma says. "Finally done. You still want some help?"

Here's your shot.

"Yeah, thanks."

Now say what you want to say.

Emma starts filing books with Steven. "Have any plans for the weekend?" she asks.

Oooh, she wants it bad . . .

"I'm not sure yet," Steven says, trying to ignore his counterpart. "How about you?"

I think we know what she wants to do . . .

"I was thinking of catching a movie tomorrow night."

Don't drop the ball . . .

"Which movie?"

Does it matter?

"I can't remember. The one where things blow up."

Your favourite kind.

"I take it your boyfriend picked it?"

"No, we broke up."

Steven and his counterpart turn towards Emma. "Really . . ."

"Yeah."

That's amazing.

"That's too bad," Steven says, putting the book in his hands on the desk.

Emma stops filing as well. "It was a long time coming."

Interesting . . .

"You seemed so happy."

"Well . . ."

The Mensa model starts imitating Emma: *"It was complicated."*

"It was kind of complicated . . ."

"I really liked him."

"I really liked him, it's just . . ."

"He didn't like himself."

"He didn't like himself, you know . . ."

"He was really insecure."

"He was really insecure, and after a while . . ."

"He started taking it out on me."

"He started taking it out on me . . ."

"I just had to end it."

"And I just had to end it."

"Oh."

Remind you of anyone?

"How are you holding up?"

"I'm all right," Emma says. "It's never easy..."

I'll translate into Honesty. She wants a rebound.

"I know what you mean," Steven says.

Good, good. Keep it coming.

"You're with someone so long..." Emma says.

"You forget what it's like to be alone."

"Yeah. Exactly."

Good. Play the "sensitive" angle.

"You forget who you were without them..." Steven says.

Okay, not that sensitive.

"...and it's takes so long to get that back."

Now you just sound like a pussy.

"I know," Emma says. "Even when you're the one who ends it."

Never mind. You two are perfect for each other.

Steven looks up at the shelves. Emma examines the list.

"Done the Es," Emma says cheerfully.

Now the Fs.

"So what's that movie about?" Steven asks.

The Mensa model hangs her head in frustration. He pretends not to notice.

"Oh, it's just a dumb action film."

Translation: "Stop asking stupid questions and ask me out."

"Who's in it?" Steven asks.

Translation: "I want to have sex with you, but I'm too much of a coward to do anything about it."

"I can't really remember."

"And it doesn't matter. I just want someone with a penis to join me."

"Uh, would you..." Steven begins.

"Yeah?"

"...uh, let me know how it is?"

Jesus.

"Oh. Sure," Emma says, clearly disappointed.

You're pathetic.

"I wouldn't get your hopes up though." Emma looks indecisively at a book, then at Steven, then down the hall. "I think I forgot something," she says. "I'll be back in a sec."

She leaves. Steven watches her walk away. The Mensa model shakes her head slowly.

"Don't say anything," Steven tells her, resuming his work.

You want to know why I dumped you? That was it.

Steven sighs. "Just because we work together doesn't mean we're soul-mates."

Ask her out, you stupid child.

"Why? Just to find out she isn't who I think she is? To find out she's like you? No, thanks."

You're a joke, you know that? All your grand aspirations, all your plans to nowhere—

"Leave me alone."

No courage. No self-respect—

"Stop it," he orders, picking up another book.

I didn't dump you. You dumped yourself. The moment you thought, "I'm not good enough," you were finished.

"Enough!" He slams the book on the ground and turns to her. "I'm a fucking librarian. I'm not Joyce. I'm not a great writer. I'm a goddamn graduate student—"

You can be whoever you—

"Bullshit! You said it yourself. My contribution to the world will be a useless analysis of an unreadable book. And I'm okay with that. You're the one who's terrified of failure, of mediocrity. I'm fine with what I am."

He goes back to work.

She continues to watch him closely. *You sure about that?*

He turns to her. "You know, there's a reason that there are a dozen new books on Joyce every year. There's a reason people write them. Even if no one reads them."

He turns away and starts working.

Emma returns with an armful of books and drops them on the table. "Almost forgot about these."

"Do you want to go out with me?" Steven asks.

Emma smiles, speechless, then laughs nervously.

Well done.

The Mensa model grins a final grin and retreats into the shadows of the stacks. Her porn-and-dildo-filled cart vanishes, along with the easy-chair in the corner and the surrounding pile of papers and books.

Emma steps towards him flirtatiously.

"Unless," Steven says, "you don't think librarians should date."

"I'm not a librarian."

"Neither am I."

Acknowledgements

Many thanks to my parents, Raf, Yash, Michael Cummings, Chris Needham, Michael Winter, and everyone else who made this book possible.